Twentieth Century

by
Ben Hecht
and Charles MacArthur

Based on a play by Charles Bruce Milholland in a
new adaptation by

Ken Ludwig

A SAMUEL FRENCH ACTING EDITION

SAMUEL
FRENCH
FOUNDED 1830
New York Hollywood London Toronto
SAMUELFRENCH.COM

ISBN 978-0-573-60299-3   Printed in U.S.A.   #22302

IMPORTANT BILLING AND CREDIT REQUIREMENTS

All producers of *TWENTIETH CENTURY* must give credit to the Author of the Play in all programs distributed in connection with performances of the Play and in all instances in which the title of the Play appears for purposes of advertising, publicizing or otherwise exploiting the Play and/or a production. The name of the Author *must* appear on a separate line on which no other name appears, immediately following the title, and *must* appear in size of type not less than fifty percent the size of the title type.

In addition, the following credit must appear in all programs ditributed in connection with the Work:

TWENTIETH CENTURY
by
Ben Hecht and Charles MacArthur
Based on a play by Charles Bruce Millholland in a new adaptation by
Ken Ludwig

This Adaptation was First Produced in New York City in 2004 by Roundabout Theatre Company. Todd Haimes, Artistic Director

Originally Produced at The Signature Theatre in 2003, Eric D. Schaeffer, Artistic Director. Sam Sweet, Managing Director. Ronnie Gunderson, Producing Director.

TWENTIETH CENTURY premiered on Broadway at the Roundabout Theatre Company's American Airlines Theatre on March 25, 2004. It was produced by The Roundabout Theatre Company, Todd Haimes, Artistc Director; Ellen Richard, Managing Director; and Julia C. Levy, Executive Director, External Affairs. It was directed by Walter Bobbie. The set was designed by John Lee Beatty, the costumes by William Ivey Long, the lighting by Peter Kaczorowski and sound by ACME Sound Partners. The hair/wig design was by Paul Huntley. The General Manager was Don-Scott Cooper, the Production Stage Manager was James Harker, the Technical Supervisor was Larry Morley, the Company Manager was Denys Baker, and casting was by Jim Carnahan, C.S.A. and Mele Nagler. The cast, in order of appearance was as follows:

ANITA HIGHLAND....................................Kellie Overbey
DR. GROVER LOCKWOOD......................Jonathan Walker
PORTER...Robert M. Jimenez
MATTHEW CLARK............................... Tom Aldredge
OWEN O'MALLEY..................................Dan Butler
CONDUCTOR....................................... Terry Beaver
IDA WEBB... Julie Halston
OSCAR JAFFE................................ Alec Baldwin
LILY GARLAND..................................Anne Heche
GEORGE SMITH...................................Ryan Shively
BEARD...Stephen DeRosa
DETECTIVE...Patrick Boll
MAX JACOBS...................................... Stephen DeRosa
RED CAPS, PASSENGERS, REPORTERS...............Patrick Boll,
                                    Todd Cerveris, Darian Dauchan,
                                    Bill English, Virginia Louise Smith

TWENTIETH CENTURY had its world premiere production in Arlington, Virginia on August 25, 2003. It was produced by the SIGNATURE THEATRE, Eric Schaeffer, Artistic Director; Sam Sweet, Managing Director; and Ronnie Gunderson, Producing Director. It was directed by Eric Schaeffer. The set was designed by James Kronzer, the costumes by Anne Kennedy, the lighting by Jonathan Blandia and sound by Toni Angelini. The hair design was by Christe Kelly and the properties were by Elsie Jones. The Assistant Director was Ronnie Gunderson, the Production Stage Manager was Sandra Barrack, and casting was by Tara Rubin Casting. The cast, in order of appearance, was as follows:

ANITA HIGHLAND...................................Rachel Gardner
DR. GROVER LOCKWOOD..............Thomas Adrian Simpson
PORTER..Rick Hammerly
OLIVER WEBB..................................... Harry A. Winter
OWEN O'MALLEY............................... Christopher Bloch
CONDUCTOR..................................... Frederick Strother
MYRTLE CLARK.................................. Donna Migliaccio
OSCAR JAFFE.. James Barbour
LILY GARLAND......................................Holly Twyford
GEORGE SMITH.....................................Will Gartshore
BEARD...Rick Hammerly
DETECTIVE.....................................Rick Hammerly
MAX JACOBS.......................................Rick Hammerly

Author's Note by Ken Ludwig

The Cast

This adaptation of *Twentieth Century* was written for performance by ten actors, 3 female, 7 male. One actor plays 4 parts – the Porter, the Beard, Max Jacobs and the Detective. Thus, the cast list is as follows:

Oscar Jaffe	Conductor
Lily Garland	Dr. Grover Lockwood
Ida Webb	Anita Highland
Owen O'Malley	Max Jacobs (doubled)
George Smith	Beard (doubled)
Matthew Clark	Detective (doubled)
	Porter (doubled)

In the world premiere production by the Signature Theatre, Rick Hammerly played Max Jacobs, the Beard, the Detective and the Porter and virtually no one in the audience knew that there was any doubling. Rick, of course, did his best to disabuse them at the curtain call.

In the Broadway production by the Roundabout Theatre Company, additional actors were hired to play the Detective and the Porter. In addition, there were actors playing a maid, a policeman and two red-caps, all to provide atmosphere. This decision was made because of the size of the stage and the resources of the company and is not in any way required.

Finally, it should be noted that in the Signature cast, Matthew Clark was named Myrtle Clark and was played by a woman. And in the original Broadway production, Ida Webb was Oliver Webb and was played by a man. The Theatre is the consummate arena to adapt to the resources available – and you should feel free to do whatever is necessary to get this play produced and create a joyful two hours.

The Set

In the original 1934 Broadway production, and in the 1952 Broadway revival, the train set did not move. The curtain rose to reveal all three rooms and all of the action took place as it would on any unit set, shifting as the action required with the aid of lighting. In both the Signature and the Roundabout productions of this adaptation, the set moved sideways, so that at any one time the audience could see only two rooms. Both approaches are equally satisfactory.

Also, the final scene of the play is meant to be played simply on the platform area in front of the train (where the opening action of the play takes place). In the Roundabout production, John Lee Beatty created a beautiful, soaring vertical "gate" for this scene. At the Signature Theatre, Jim Kronzer ingeniously created a "skin" which looked like the outside of the train car and slid into place for the opening and closing scenes of the play. However, the simple stage area in front of the train with nothing but the open train in the background works equally well.

Preface by Ken Ludwig

This play came about thanks to a wonderful man named Roger Stevens. Roger was a great Broadway producer and – at the time I got to know him in the late 1980s – the Chairman of the Kennedy Center for the Performing Arts. At this time, the Kennedy Center was producing one of my early plays, *Sullivan and Gilbert*, which was the last play Roger produced in his capacity as Chairman before he retired.

During the weeks leading up to the production, Roger and I became warm friends. He was one of those truly great men that we all hope to have as a friend: wise, avuncular, funny; and he cared as deeply about the theatre as anyone I have ever known. Typically, I would wander into his office around noon and wait happily while he finished up business. Then we'd muse about life and the theatre for an hour; and sometimes we'd go to lunch. As a young playwright, I simply loved being anywhere in this giant's orbit. He'd point to a picture on the wall from one of his *hundreds* of Broadway productions – Lunt and Fontanne in *The Visit;* or Ralph Richardson in *The Waltz of the Toreadors* – then he'd tell an anecdote about "Larry" or "Viven" or "Helen" – always in a way that made me feel part of this great tradition; as though Larry and Vivien would have been thrilled to have me as a colleague. Looking back, I know that Roger was aware of the effect he was having on me, and that it amused him in a genuinely fatherly way.

One day, as Roger and I gazed up at the library of plays he kept in his office, he put his hand on my shoulder and said, "Kenny, I think you should take a look at this." He pulled down a volume entitled *The Plays of Charles MacArthur*. "Take it with you. It's a present."

At home that night, I devoured the entire volume. I knew *The Front Page*, of course. But I didn't know the others; and I was struck at the time by one in particular, *Twentieth Century*. Funny, fast, touching, theatrical. I loved it. The next day in his office, I learned that the play had last been performed on Broadway in the early 1950s with Jose Ferrer and Gloria Swanson. I was intrigued. However, about this time, preparations for

Sullivan and Gilbert were heating up, and I put the book aside and forgot about it.

Fifteen years later, I was in that agonizing state of being called "between plays." By this time I had several Broadway plays under my belt, including *Lend Me A Tenor, Crazy For You,* and *Moon Over Buffalo.* I had just finished staging *Moon* at the Old Vic in London with Joan Collins and Frank Langella. And I was tying myself in knots trying to come up with an idea for a new play. The Kennedy Center was back in my life at that moment – they were playing my musical adaptation of *Tom Sawyer* – and perhaps that's why, in perusing my shelves for an idea, I plucked down the MacArthur volume and started to reread it. An hour later I had an idea. *Twentieth Century.* It had everything I love about classic comedies: a great comic premise; an interesting story with a strong motor; larger-than-life characters; rip-roaring set pieces that are genuinely funny; and a touching romance in the center of it all.

I did some research and found out that *Twentieth Century* hadn't been done on Broadway since that Ferrer-Swanson outing in the 1950s. And then I found it that it was rarely done by *anybody.* Indeed, it was out of print. I reread the play and realized instantly why it was so neglected: it called for 28 actors. And *nobody* produces a straight play with 28 actors any more. You might get away with 10 or 12, if you're lucky. So I got to thinking: What if I wrote an adaptation for, say, 10 actors. I knew I could retain the spirit of the piece. But could I retain the atmosphere and the stunning architecture? I thought I could.

That very day, I contacted James MacArthur, son of Charles MacArthur and Helen Hayes. I told him about my idea and he was supportive from the first minute. All his life he has proudly championed the great theatrical legacies of both of his adored parents, and he was thrilled with the idea of giving *Twentieth Century* a new life. From that moment on, Jim has been the greatest of boosters, the best of critics and the nicest of friends – and I'm happy to thank him now, in print, for all his help in bringing *Twentieth Century* back to the audience it deserves.

Once I'd finished writing the adaptation, the next step was getting it produced. I sent it to my good friend Eric Schaeffer, and he immediately agreed to produce it – and direct it – at his own theatre, one of the most creative, adventurous theatre spaces on Earth, The Signature Theatre in Arlington, Virginia. It starred James Barbour and Holly Twyford and was a bona fide hit. By this time, my friend Walter Bobbie had read a copy of the play, and he offered it, with my blessing, to Todd Haimes and the Roundabout Theatre for a Broadway outing. We opened on Broadway in March of 2004 with Alec Baldwin and Anne Heche in the leads. Again, we were a hit, and the play was virtually sold out for its entire run.

Ever since these two productions opened, I'm frequently asked the same question: Did I make a lot of changes in the text of the original script? The answer is that in cutting the cast from 28 to 10, I had to. Indeed, I'd say that at least 50% of the dialogue on the following pages is mine, including some entire scenes, while the other 50% is pure Hecht and MacArthur. But my goal has always been to retain the essence and exuberance of the original: the sly wit, the smart-mouthed commentary, the outsized egos and the relentless plot. With the memory of Roger Stevens in mind, I hope I've succeeded.

Ken Ludwig
Washington, DC

For Mom and Dad, always

Ken

ACT I

ANNOUNCER'S VOICE. *(In the dark, over a loud speaker.)* Attention, please, Twentieth Century Limited for New York and Boston now ready on Track 14. All aboard!

(The lights come up on the interior of the Twentieth Century Limited just before departure from La Salle Street Station, Chicago. The time is March, 1933.

We see three compartments on the train. From left to right: Drawing Room B, Drawing Room A, and the Observation Car. The two Drawing Rooms each have a door at the back, leading to a corridor that runs along the back of the train. This corridor leads to the main entry door of the Observation Car. Most communication between these three rooms is along the corridor and through these doors.

In addition, there is a door connecting the two Drawing Rooms, along the common wall – although this door is normally kept locked. Also, along the outer wall, Drawing Room B has a door leading to the bedroom.

The Twentieth Century Limited is spacious and beautifully appointed. Each drawing room has chairs, a writing desk,

13

mirrors, lamps, curtains, etc. The Observation Car is essentially a lounge, with an open central area and some easy chairs. Our first impression as the lights come up is one of hustle and bustle up and down the corridor and through the rooms and the Observation Car. For purposes of this opening, we might see the platform as well.)

CONDUCTOR. Attention, please, Twentieth Century Limited for New York and Boston now ready on Track 14. All aboard!

(After a moment, we meet DR. GROVER LOCKWOOD and his somewhat younger companion, ANITA HIGHLAND. LOCKWOOD normally projects an air of confidence, but at the moment, he's a nervous wreck. ANITA is his attractive, down-to-earth office manager who's ready for some excitement in her life. They both carry luggage; and the PORTER, an efficient fellow who knows his job, is just approaching them.)

ANITA. I've got to admit, this is exciting, Grover.
PORTER. May we take your bags, sir? Madam?
ANITA. Why thank you, Porter. That's very kind.
PORTER. And you're in?
DR. LOCKWOOD. *(Checking the tickets.)* Drawing Room A, Car 186.
PORTER. *(Taking their luggage.)* I'll meet you there.
DR. LOCKWOOD. Good, good ...

(ANITA and GROVER whisper as they move away:)

ANITA. Stop making faces, Grover. Nobody saw us get on the train.

DR. LOCKWOOD. If my wife knew about this, she'd take every penny ...

ANITA. Grover, would you please stop worrying and just relax! Try to smile.

(He does.)

DR. LOCKWOOD. How do I look?

ANITA. Like you've been electrocuted.

(They exit.

By this time, MATTHEW CLARK has entered carrying a black leather satchel and a Bible. He's in late middle age, an odd little man, pale and upright, neatly dressed in an old-fashioned suit and tie.)

PORTER. May I help you with your bag, sir?

CLARK. Oh, no no no. No no. No thank you. *(He hold the satchel to his chest.)* It's very kind of you to offer, though. Very charitable. Do you read the Bible?

PORTER. Yes sir, I do.

CLARK. In that case, here's a dollar for you.

PORTER. Thank you, sir!

CLARK. Do you read it every day?

PORTER. I have to admit I don't sir.

CLARK. Then I'll take the dollar back.

(He does, then walks away. The Porter watches him, puzzled, then heads straight to Drawing Room A.)

ANNOUNCER. *(On loud speaker.)* Track 14! Twentieth Century! All aboard!

(By this time, the PORTER has reached Drawing Room A. ANITA and LOCKWOOD follow him in.)

ANITA. Well this looks nice and comfortable.

PORTER. *(To LOCKWOOD.)* And may I have your name, please?

DR. LOCKWOOD. *(Panicked)*... My-my name? ...What for?

PORTER. It's customary, sir, in case you get any telegrams.

DR. LOCKWOOD. Oh. Why, it's uh ... I'm glad you asked me that, because uh ... generally, I find that it's not something that generally gets ...

ANITA. Dr. Grover C. Lockwood.

DR. LOCKWOOD. *(Hoarsely)* Right. And wife. Mrs. Doctor. Lockwood. Mrs. Lockwood. I'm the doctor. She's the wife. We're married.

PORTER. Thank you very much.

(He exits, closing the door.)

ANITA. That was very smooth, Grover. Now they'll never suspect a thing.

DR. LOCKWOOD. Are you crazy! Giving out my name?!

ANITA. I had to say something. You just stood there.

DR. LOCKWOOD. Oh God, if my wife knew about this ...

ANITA. Why don't you talk about your wife some more, Grover. Or better still, you could pull out her picture and have a good cry.

*(They cuddle up together, as —
The action moves to the Observation car, where OWEN O'MAL-*

LEY is arguing with the PORTER. O'MALLEY is a harassed and bellicose Irishman, not without a certain charm and even poesy. He is cynical and assured, but disposed to fight about anything at the drop of a nuance.)

O'MALLEY. You've got a lot of nerve, you foul Corsican!

PORTER. I only asked to see your ticket.

O'MALLEY. And I told you to put them bags into Drawing Room A before I flatten you. Mr. Jaffe needs that room.

PORTER. But there's somebody in there already!

O'MALLEY. Then throw 'em out! They don't belong there, trust me!

PORTER. *(Intimidated)* Well maybe there's a mistake or something. I'll go see.

O'MALLEY. I'll go with you.

CONDUCTOR. *(Offstage)* Track 14. All aboard!

(The Porter heads for Drawing Room A and O'MALLEY follows. The lights come up in A and we see LOCKWOOD in a clinch with ANITA. The buzzer sounds and LOCKWOOD jumps.)

DR. LOCKWOOD. Yes?! Who is it?

PORTER. *(Off)* Porter.

DR. LOCKWOOD. Wait! …Just a minute …! *(He straightens his hair and tie.)* All right, come in.

PORTER. *(Entering)* Beg pardon, sir, but can I see your tickets?

DR. LOCKWOOD. Why certainly.

ANITA. What is it Grover? Darling.

DR. LOCKWOOD. Porter?

PORTER. Gentleman here say's it's his room.

DR. LOCKWOOD. It is not!

O'MALLEY. Oh it isn't, huh? Well tell me something. Do you lift weights? Huh? Have you got any muscles on them bones?!

DR. LOCKWOOD. *(Thrown)* Well, not really …

O'MALLEY. Then step outside. We'll settle this like real men.

ANITA. Grover, he's drunk. I can smell it from here.

O'MALLEY. That's a lie! Not a drop has touched these lips in over ten minutes!

PORTER. *(Hurrying away.)* I'll call the conductor.

O'MALLEY. Fine! Call the conductor! Call the whole damn orchestra! *(To LOCKWOOD.)* I'll take care of you and that alleged squaw of yours later.

(He heads back to the Observation Car, where the PORTER is having a whispered conversation with the CONDUCTOR – a dignified specimen in a tailcoat with a heavy gold watch chain.)

PORTER. That's the gentleman there.

CONDUCTOR. All right, I'll attend to him. *(Coldly, to O'MALLEY.)* What seems to be the trouble, young man?

O'MALLEY. "Young man." You call me a "young man?" I'll have to give you a kiss for that one.

CONDUCTOR. Get away from me! Now listen here -

O'MALLEY. No, you listen, General. There's a pair of foul turtle-doves in Drawing Room A, and I've got to shoo 'em out before Mr. Jaffe gets here.

CONDUCTOR. *(Thawing)* Do you mean Oscar Jaffe., the theatrical man?

O'MALLEY. The earth-shaker himself. I'm his Press Agent. Now let's have some action.

CONDUCTOR. May I see your ticket?

O'MALLEY. How many times do I have to go over this? I ain't got a ticket!

CONDUCTOR. Then I'm afraid you're out of luck, Mr. Jaffe. or no Mr. Jaffe.

O'MALLEY. Listen, you keep this up and I'll EAT THEM BUTTONS OFF YOUR COAT!!

(IDA WEBB enters and begins to function at once. IDA is a tough, efficient, smart-mouthed dame who plays poker with the boys – and wins. She's been married three or four times – she can't remember which – but since none of the men were as tough or romantic as she is, she sent them packing.)

WEBB. Owen, is everything all fixed?

O'MALLEY. NO! Diplomacy ain't workin'! *(To CONDUCTOR.)* This is Miss Ida Webb, Jaffe's general manager and fixer-upper. Ida, fix him up.

CONDUCTOR. Now listen you – !

WEBB. Owen, what's the problem?

O'MALLEY. Oscar wants room A. There's somebody in there already and he won't throw 'em out!

WEBB. Why Room A?

O'MALLEY. I have no idea, but Oscar says it's life and death.

WEBB. I see. Right. Conductor. Take a telegram.

CONDUCTOR. *(Flustered)* A telegram …?

WEBB. To Mr. A. L. Johnson, Vice-President, New York Central Line. "My Dear Albert –" (*At these magic words, the Conductor turns white.)* "I'm having some difficulty getting proper service on the Century in charge of Conductor –" What's your name?

CONDUCTOR. Listen, Miss Webb…

WEBB. *(Coldly)* Well, speak up.

CONDUCTOR. There's no use wiring anybody about this. I'm perfectly willing to give Mr. Jaffe every consideration – I've carried Mr. Jaffe before – but you'll have to make your own arrangements with the people in A.

WEBB. Happy to, Conductor. Who is in A?

PORTER. A Dr. and Mrs. Lockwood.

O'MALLEY. Dr. and Mrs. Hell! It's Romeo and Juliet without the blood test.

WEBB. Come on, Owen.

(They cross to Drawing Room A and sound the buzzer – at which point we see LOCKWOOD and ANITA entwined.)

DR. LOCKWOOD. Oh, now what?!

O'MALLEY. *(Thumping on the door.)* Open the door.

ANITA. *(Frightened)* My God!

DR. LOCKWOOD. Don't get rattled. You'll give everything away. *(He opens the door, taking an outraged air.)* What's the idea of this continual intrusion?

WEBB. Are you Dr. Lockwood?

DR. LOCKWOOD. Yes! Who are you?

WEBB. And is this lady here Mrs. Lockwood?

ANITA. Conductor, I'm beginning to feel persecuted.

WEBB. I'll be right back.

O'MALLEY. Where are you going?

WEBB. I'm going to call up his real wife and have a chat. The poor little thing.

DR. LOCKWOOD. *(Panic-Stricken)* Just a minute! Please! Wait!

WEBB. On the other hand, we don't really want to cause any

trouble, now do we, Owen?

O'MALLEY. Not me. I hate conflict.

WEBB. Look, doctor, I've got two tickets here, an upper and lower two cars ahead. The difference in price is fifteen dollars in your favor. We'll call it twenty.

(She peels off $20 and hands it to LOCKWOOD along with the tickets.)

WEBB. Here you are.

DR. LOCKWOOD. *(Astounded)* What?

WEBB. I strongly advise you to take it. There will be no more questions.

ANITA. *(In rage)* Are you going to stand for this, Grover?

DR. LOCKWOOD. It'll be all right, honey. Come on.

ANITA. But Grover – !

DR. LOCKWOOD. Don't argue with me! Porter, bring the bags!

PORTER. Yes sir!

(LOCKWOOD drags ANITA out, and the CONDUCTOR and PORTER follow.)

O'MALLEY. Bye, honey.

(WEBB. and O'MALLEY remain in A, closing the door.)

O'MALLEY. Okay, we got the room. Now all we need is Oscar.

WEBB. I'd like to know what he would ever do without us.

O'MALLEY. I'm glad you fixed the train. Now why don't

you fix one of his plays?

WEBB. "Joan of Arc." That was his biggest turkey yet.

O'MALLEY. I didn't know whether to watch it or stuff it and serve it with cranberries.

WEBB. That's three flops in a row. We haven't had a hit since Lily left him.

WEBB. I told him Joan of Arc wouldn't run a week. Right to his face I told him. I said people don't want to see some dame in an iron petticoat. *(O'MALLEY has pulled out a liquor flask.)* Hey. You said you weren't going to take a drink on this train.

O'MALLEY. I conquered my will power.

(A knock on the door.)

WEBB. Come in!

(LOCKWOOD enters.)

DR. LOCKWOOD. Excuse me …?

O'MALLEY. *(Rising)* You, again.

DR. LOCKWOOD. Wait! The Porter said … Is it true you're with Oscar Jaffe? The big producer?

WEBB. That's right.

DR. LOCKWOOD. Well, I … *(Proudly)* I've written a play!

O'MALLEY. Oy vey …

DR. LOCKWOOD. *(Pulling out a copy)* Could you show it to him? When he arrives? I'd really appreciate it.

WEBB. I don't think Mr. Jaffe would be interested right now.

DR. LOCKWOOD. Oh, he'll be interested in this play, I guarantee it. It's unique. It's about … Joan of Arc.
Listen. You've got to admit, you owe me a favor. Right? I'll tell you what, I'll come back later. Then he can decide. Okay? All

right?

WEBB. Fine, come back later.

DR. LOCKWOOD. Thanks … fellow Thespians.

(As WEBB closes the door on LOCKWOOD –

– the actions shifts to the Observation Car, as MATTHEW CLARK hurries in. He looks sharply in both directions to make sure he's alone, then he calls out:)

CLARK. Repent! For the time is at hand!

(He begins slapping round, colorful stickers on the windows and pulls the shades down to cover them. The stickers say: "Repent for the time is at hand!" As he does this, he sings:)

CLARK.
"Take my hand, take my hand,
Take me to the promised land,
Blessed Jesus, O blessed Jesus.
Take my hand, take my hand,
Take me to the promised land …

(The CONDUCTOR enters, followed by the PORTER, and CLARK stops abruptly, hiding his stickers. The CONDUCTOR calls out:)

CONDUCTOR. Last call! All aboard! Last call!

(In Drawing Room A, WEBB. jumps up.)

WEBB. Oh my God!

(She and O'MALLEY rush into the Observation Car.)

WEBB. *(Wildly)* Just a minute! Hold it, Conductor. Stop! Stop!

CONDUCTOR. What's the matter?

WEBB. You can't start the train yet! Mr. Jaffe isn't on board!

CONDUCTOR. Sorry, this train waits for no man. Not while I'm alive.

O'MALLEY. That sounds like a solution to me.

(Suddenly, the train gives a lurch – putting WEBB and O'MALLEY into an even greater panic.)

WEBB. Owen, do something!

O'MALLEY. Where's the emergency rope?

PORTER. You can't touch that!

O'MALLEY. There it is!

WEBB. Grab it, Owen!

CONDUCTOR. Stop that right now! Porter! Stop him!

(As they struggle, WEBB pulls out a pad and pencil and starts writing a wire – trying to frighten the CONDUCTOR. The following five speeches are spoken simultaneously:)

WEBB. To A.L. Johnson, Vice-President, New York Central Line …

CONDUCTOR. You can wire God Almighty if you want to! This train starts now and on time and I am not to be intimidated!

WEBB. Dear Al … How are the wife and kids! I regret to inform you of the behavior of one of your so-called Conductors -

PORTER. *(Struggling)* Let go of that bell rope! I'm warning you! That'll send ya to prison, sure as shootin'!

O'MALLEY. Get off o' me, you foul Corsican! This train is goin' no place till Mr. Jaffe gets here if I have to stand in front of it!

(As the argument continues, OSCAR JAFFE. enters Drawing Room A. He goes straight to the door communicating with Drawing Room B and tries to open it, but it's locked. He rattles the handle, but it won't open – and so he starts screaming at the top of his lungs:)

JAFFE. *(Cutting through all the noise)* OWEN, IDA, GET ME A PORTER! *(WEBB and O'MALLEY stop cold and look up.)* I WANT A PORTER THIS INSTANT!

O'MALLEY. My God! The earth-shaker's on board.

WEBB. It's okay, Conductor. Sorry for the trouble. Porter, come with me!

(WEBB, O'MALLEY and the PORTER hurry to Drawing Room A. As they go – and as the CONDUCTOR mops his brow – we have a moment to look at the great OSCAR JAFFE. He is a man in his prime, in a fur-collared coat equipped with frogs across the chest and wearing a black velour hat and Windsor tie. He carries a cane of black ebony with a silver tip, once the property of the late Edwin Booth. He lives, breathes, eats and dreams about the theatre and nothing else.
It should be noted at this point that MR. JAFFE's voice, when he isn't screaming, is a lofty instrument, designed to meet the great moments in life. It is sibilant and judicial. Behind its measured beat is a continual tremolo of emotion. When MR. JAFFE. speaks he gives the effect of one who is playing his

*simplest words on a Cremona cello. Fate and Weltschmertz lie
behind the most accidental of the JAFFE utterances. He is an
Actor.)*

O'MALLEY. *(Entering)* Hello, Maestro. Welcome to the
Titanic.

WEBB. Here's your Porter, Oscar.

JAFFE. How do you do, young man, it's a pleasure to be rid-
ing on your magnificent railroad. Now open this door.

PORTER. I'm afraid that's against the rules, sir.

JAFFE. Ida, have you got five dollars?

WEBB. No.

JAFFE. Liar. Just give it to him. I'll reimburse you.

O'MALLEY. He can pay you back with tickets for "Joan of
Arc."

JAFFE. Go ahead, Porter. It's all right.

*(The PORTER takes the money and unlocks the door to Drawing
Room B. JAFFE peeks in, sees no one there and goes right in.)*

JAFFE. It's empty.

PORTER. Yes sir.

JAFFE. Wasn't it reserved?

PORTER. Yes sir, maybe the party's getting on at Englewood.
Lots of 'em do.

JAFFE. And when do we arrive in Englewood, pray tell?

PORTER. About ten minutes.

JAFFE. Good. Thank you, Porter. You may go. (*The PORTER
exits.*) Owen. Where are the flowers?

O'MALLEY. What flowers?

JAFFE. I distinctly told you to bank Drawing Room B with
gardenias. I sent word to the box office.

O'MALLEY. The box office? Well, what would I be doing around there?! With sixteen process servers lying in ambush for us. I can get arrested all by myself, thank you.

JAFFE. *(The good shepherd.)* You'll have to stop drinking, Owen. You're no good to me this way, it's discouraging. Ida, wire Maurice the florist in Toledo to send all the gardenias he has to this car. I want a card with a message. Let me think … "To the little lady of the snows…" No. I used that last time. Just a minute … "From the grave of someone you loved yesterday." How's that?

O'MALLEY. That's nice and cheerful.

JAFFE. It's perfect. Why can't I get a few playwrights to write like that?

WEBB. You did. That's why we're out of money.

(The three walk back into Drawing Room A, closing the connecting door behind them.)

JAFFE. Owen, go order lunch. I'm famished.

O'MALLEY. The diner's packed.

JAFFE. Tell them it's for me. See that they put me by myself at a very large table.

O'MALLEY. If you want privacy why don't you travel in a balloon?

(O'MALLEY exits.)

JAFFE. What started O'Malley drinking again? Is it a woman?

WEBB. Yeah, it's a woman. "Joan of Arc."

JAFFE. Do you know what I was thinking on my way to the train? I was thinking that of all my sixty-eight productions the most beautiful was "Joan of Arc." I cried like a baby at every performance.

WEBB. So did I, but for a different reason.

JAFFE. That fire effect I did at the end was pure genius.

WEBB. So was that disappearing trick where you made the audience vanish.

JAFFE. Well I liked it!

WEBB. I'm glad, because we lost seventy-four thousand dollars on it.

JAFFE. *(Awed by his own greatness.)* God, what a magnificent failure! If I am a genius, Ida, it's because of my failures. Always remember that.

WEBB. I'll put it on a sign and you can wear it on street corners holding a little cup: "I'm a genius, please feed me." Now listen, Oscar, this trip from Chicago to New York takes sixteen hours, we arrive at Grand Central at nine tomorrow morning and the banks open at ten –

JAFFE. Don't worry me about money right now, do you mind?

WEBB. Oscar, listen! If we don't find some cash by tomorrow, they're going to take the Jaffe Theatre, and I'm not kidding.

JAFFE. They wouldn't dare.

WEBB. They issued a writ on Friday.

JAFFE. *(The one subject that makes him go totally wild.)* And who do you think is behind it, huh?! I'll tell you who!

WEBB. Boss –

JAFFE. Max Jacobs! That so-called producer! That cheap little crook I picked out of the gutter! I gave him life and he betrayed me! Don't you remember? When I fired him he said he'd have his revenge.

WEBB. Oscar, it's not Max Jacobs. It's the banks. All the banks. They got together last week.

JAFFE. They did, huh? Well, I'll tell you something, Ida. Skies were never bluer. Who do you think is getting on the train at Englewood. Hm? I'll give you a hint. She's an old friend of ours. She has bright blonde hair and sparkling eyes, she's five foot six with a splendid figure, and if she ever fell into a swamp and met a starving crocodile, she'd strangle him, turn him inside out and make him into a purse with matching shoes.

WEBB. Lily Garland?

JAFFE. Right!

WEBB. She's coming back with us?

JAFFE. You bet she is! Ha ha! Starring in my next production. Back in the fold where she belongs.

WEBB. Oh my God. That's the best news I've heard in years.

JAFFE. I knew you'd like it.

WEBB. When you split up with Lily I never opened my yap, but I just knew you were cutting your throat.

JAFFE. So you thought I was through, eh? Well let me tell you something. That is when I'm at my best, my girl. With my back against the wall. Disaster staring me in the face. "Henry the Eighth." "The Bride of Baghdad." "Chaim Pipick." They had me down, but I'm like a prize-fighter, up at the count of nine, can he get to his feet?, he staggers for a moment, can he recover?, then swings with the fury of a wounded lion. Ha ha!

WEBB. I'll tell you one thing. When those bankers see her name on a contract, they'll be giving us money. We can write our own ticket. She's the biggest draw in the country!

JAFFE. And now we have compartments next to each other. That's why I needed Drawing Room A.

WEBB. So that was it.

JAFFE. Now here's my plan. I want you to bump into her, accidentally, and tell her I have in hand the most unbelievable new

play with a part that fits her like a glove. Half-devil, half-woman.
The greatest character ever put on stage.

WEBB. Wow! What's the play?

JAFFE. I have no idea. Now I'll have to find somebody who
can write it. Remind me to find out if Bertolt Brecht is available.

WEBB. Oscar –

JAFFE. Or maybe that new chap, Noel Coward. We could add
music –

WEBB. Osc –

JAFFE. Or Ibsen. Find out if he's still alive –

WEBB. Oscar, listen! Have you got Lily under contract or
not?

JAFFE. Don't get technical on me, Ida.

WEBB. But it's the contract that'll make all the difference!

JAFFE. Oh, she'll sign for me. I created her.

WEBB. Was she glad to see you at least?

JAFFE. See me when? I haven't seen her for years.

WEBB. Oscar!! Oh my God!!

JAFFE. Oh, stop worrying. I'll get her signed up. And remember – I never closed the iron door on her.

WEBB. Oscar, listen to me – Would you just listen! The banks
will not stop foreclosing on your assets until they actually see her
name on a contract. In black and white. Signed.

JAFFE. I understand that. Which is why you will bump into
Lily accidentally and tell her I'm on the train. She'll be ecstatic,
but she'll try to hide it. And tell her the part in question is promised to Loretta Young. She hates her. It was Loretta she caught me
in bed with. *(Dreamily)* It broke her heart.

WEBB. Loretta Young?

JAFFE. I told her that Shirley Temple was our love child.

WEBB. She's going to be pretty snooty after the hit she's
made.

JAFFE. What hit?

WEBB. The movies!

JAFFE. She'll never be any good in the movies.

WEBB. What are you talking about? She won the gold statue.

JAFFE. What gold statue?

WEBB. A gold statue that some academy gives away every year, for best performance. They're calling her another Marlene Dietrich.

JAFFE. That's impossible. She can't be any good in the movies. She's got a face like a soft shell crab. It took me four years to make her look vaguely human.

WEBB. Listen, Oscar, as long as the Lily Garland thing isn't definite, I've got something to suggest. I got a telegram this morning from Max Jacobs.

JAFFE. Looking for a job, I suppose.

WEBB. Max wired me of his own accord –

JAFFE. I forbid you ever to mention the name Max Jacobs to me again. That's final! Besides, his real name is Mandelbaum. Max Mandelbaum. He started out selling herring on 34th Street till they arrested him for unclean practices. I fired him for stealing.

WEBB. Oscar, you fired him because of "Carmen."

JAFFE. Who's Carmen?

WEBB. The opera "Carmen?" The one you produced together. You insisted on putting a real bull on stage.

JAFFE. He was a magnificent animal.

WEBB. He fell into the orchestra pit! They had to shoot him in front of the audience!

JAFFE. That was tragic.

WEBB. You had him ground up into hamburgers!

JAFFE. I was trying to salvage our investment!

WEBB. That's not the point! The point is, Max disagreed with you.

JAFFE. The point is, what does Max Jacobs know about the theatre!

WEBB. He knows enough to produce three straight hits in a row while you've been laying one egg after another. That's just facts!

JAFFE. I've had enough of your treachery. Get out of my sight!

WEBB. Just listen to this wire.

JAFFE. You've shown your true colors, now get out! You're fired! You're like Brutus in the marketplace, stabbing the only man who was ever good to you! Go to Mandlebaum and sell herring together!

WEBB. Oscar –

JAFFE. Out! Out! Out! You traitor! I close the iron door on you!

(JAFFE who has backed WEBB through the door, slams it in her face.

A train passes with a mighty roar, and the action shifts to the Observation Car. The CONDUCTOR and ANITA are having an animated discussion. MATTHEW CLARK sits nearby looking on with interest.)

ANITA. *(Sightly hysterical)* It was awful! I hardly knew what was happening! I was sitting reading a magazine when all of a sudden I felt something hit me on the head!

CONDUCTOR. Did you see anyone go by?

ANITA. No. But when I took my hat off, this sticker was on it. Look! "Repent for the time is at hand."

CONDUCTOR. That's the one. There's hundreds of 'em, all over the train.

CLARK. I'm sure whoever's doing it means no harm.

CONDUCTOR. Maybe. Or he could be some crackpot with a

gun.

CLARK. Oh, Lord, I certainly hope not.

(He exits.)

ANITA. I just don't understand it, Conductor. First it was the drawing room, now this. It isn't fair!

CONDUCTOR. I can assure you, madam, it's just a coincidence. Unless that Jaffe and his crew have something to do with it. And I wouldn't put it past them –

ANITA. Conductor, look!

(WEBB has just entered from the direction that Clark exited – and she has an identical sticker on her hat, to which she's oblivious.)

ANITA. *(Wispering)* I'll bet she did it.

CONDUCTOR. *(Vengefuly)* That wouldn't surprise me in the least. *(Approaching WEBB.)* Well, my good woman, this time you've gone too far.

WEBB. I beg your pardon.

CONDUCTOR. Oh, you don't know what I'm talking about, huh? What's that on your hat?

(The CONDUCTOR tries to get WEBB's hat and WEBB fights him off.)

WEBB. Keep your hands off me!

CONDUCTOR. Give me that!

WEBB. What the hell is going on here?!

CONDUCTOR. You're going right through this train with soap and a pail of hot water and take every one of these sticker down!

WEBB. "Repent for the time is at hand?" You're nuttier than a fruit cake. What the hell would I be doing with stickers? I've got enough trouble.

PORTER. *(Entering from hallway, excitedly to the CONDUCTOR.)* Conductor! Conductor! Somebody just went through the dining car, this minute, and stuck 'em on all the windows!

CONDUCTOR. Did you see him?

PORTER. No, sir. Just the back of him. He's heading towards the caboose!

CONDUCTOR. Come on. He won't get away this time. *(To WEBB.)* Sorry, Miss. I guess you're not guilty. This time

(The CONDUCTOR and the PORTER race out. O'MALLEY enters and sees IDA sitting there and looks at her quizzically, wondering why she isn't with JAFFE.)

WEBB. He closed the iron door.

(A train whistle sounds, as O'MALLEY continues to Drawing Room A. JAFFE is alone, as O'MALLEY comes through the door.)

O'MALLEY. Hey, boss, where's Ida?

JAFFE. Miss Webb. is no longer with us. There are only two musketeers left now, but we'll fight all the harder. Like Damon and Pythias. Robin Hood and Little John. Sherlock Holmes and a slightly drunken Doctor Watson. Now take out your pad and sit down. First, I want you to wire all the dramatic editors in New

York and tell them that I closed "Joan of Arc" as a gesture.

O'MALLEY. A gesture of what?

JAFFE. Of defiance. Because the play was unworthy of me.

O'MALLEY. Shows what I know. I thought it was because the play stank.

JAFFE. You have no soul, Owen. There were beautiful moments in that play.

O'MALLEY. I'm sure you're right. I saw it at a disadvantage. My seat was facing the stage.

(The buzzer sounds.)

JAFFE. That's Ida, coming to beg my forgiveness. Tell her to go.

(DR. LOCKWOOD enters.)

DR. LOCKWOOD. Dr. Jaffe.?

JAFFE. Yes?

DR. LOCKWOOD. How do you do? I'm Dr. Lockwood.

JAFFE. Did you send for a doctor, Owen?

DR. LOCKWOOD. No, I'm here in a private capacity. I ... have written a play, sir, especially for you. It's called ... "Joan of Arc." *(JAFFE reacts.)* You see, by day I may be a doctor, but at night, alone in my bedroom, using nothing but a simple pen, I explore my inner reaches.

JAFFE. I don't want to even think about that.

DR. LOCKWOOD. Will you read it?! You must! It's magnificent! I've taken a whole new approach to the subject. You see, I've given Joan a friend, a strong, dedicated man she can rely on. The kind of man every girl dreams of. A doctor!

JAFFE. Give the play to my secretary. I'll read it later.

DR. LOCKWOOD. *(Giving it to O'MALLEY.)* Take good care of it. It's the only copy in the world.

O'MALLEY. I'll memorize it, Doc.

JAFFE. Don't be funny, Owen. A play is a sacred trust. It is the earth in which the rest of us grow.

DR. LOCKWOOD. Thank you, Mr. Jaffe.

JAFFE. You're welcome. Now if you don't mind, I'm very busy. *(LOCKWOOD exits.)* Flush that thing down the toilet, Owen. *(O'MALLEY throws it into the bathroom and closes the door.)* Owen, did you read that telegram from Max Jacobs?

O'MALLEY. I sure did.

JAFFE. What did it say?

OWEN. He wants you to direct a new play for him, and he said he'd give you ten percent.

JAFFE. "Give me?" "Give me?!" The man is in an opium stupor. He takes drugs! I never told you that part. He's a drug addict. Take a wire, Owen. "To Max Jacobs, né Mandelbaum: I have it on good authority that you carry more diseases on your body than are believed to exist on the Asian continent – "

O'MALLEY. It'll never get through.

JAFFE. All right, start again. "Dear Max: You are the foulest, most vile, putrid piece of trash that ever walked this earth – and I say that with all due respect. In reply to your impudent offer, I am holding open your old job as office boy, feeling that you will need it when even that part of the public which enjoys filth in the theatre has been nauseated beyond endurance by your degenerate offerings!"

O'MALLEY. That'll teach him not to point.

CONDUCTOR. *(Off)* Englewood! Now arriving Englewood, Illinois!

(JAFFE freezes. He holds his heart in pain, looks up and sighs deeply. This is it.)

JAFFE. *(Hoarsely)* Owen ... she's getting on here ... Lily ... Lily Garland.

O'MALLEY. Lily's back?

JAFFE. I've tried for years to tear her out of my brain, but I've failed. She's in here, eating at my heart like some grey rat. Owen, when I love a woman I'm an Oriental. It never goes. It never dies. The only way I can breathe again is to get her back. *(With something like hatred.)* Make her pay for what she's done to me.

O'MALLEY. If she doesn't throw her arms around you the minute she sees you, she's a bigger fool than I ever thought she was.

JAFFE. Irishman, once in a blue moon you say just the right thing. We've stopped.

CONDUCTOR. *(Off)* Englewood!

JAFFE. Let's go to the platform and watch her get on. Shh. We've got to be Indians.

(They exit. As the train pulls in, we hear voices calling "Telegrams!" "Newspaper!" "Car 186!" "Red Cap!" etc.
The lights come up on Drawing Room B. LILY GARLAND opens the door with a dramatic gesture. LILY is a kind of female OSCAR JAFFE – stunning, histrionic, glamorous, egotistical and totally magnetic. She's used to being pampered, getting her own way and being told that she's the center of the universe. In short, she's a Star.)

LILY. *(The tragedienne; to the world; strewing her gloves and at on the floor.)* My God, my God, my God. Another compartment.

Another lonely room. No one cares if I'm...*(She leans her head into the corridor and yells.)*... Lily Garland! *(She enters the room.)* All they want is more of me. More, more. I could be a rag doll, or an animal in a circus. *(She pulls her Academy Award out of her purse and admires it.)* What do they care? Oh, God, I'm so tired.

(GEORGE SMITH, her agent and current lover, enters. GEORGE is a collar ad with temperament. Not bright, but tenacious. He's considerably younger than LILY.)

GEORGE. You poor thing.

LILY. Why do I do it, George? It's not for the money. I despise money. I despise all those trappings, those baubles, those symbols of emptiness ...Where's my luggage?

GEORGE. The Porter said it'll be right in.

LILY. All of my jewelry is in there!

GEORGE. Lily, it's fine –

LILY. The necklace that Louis Mayer gave me. The tiara – !

GEORGE. Lily –

LILY. I put you in charge of the luggage, you blockhead! That jewelry is worth a fortune!

GEORGE. *(Holding up his briefcase.)* Lily, I have your jewelry right here! I kept it separate.

LILY. Oh, George, don't ever scare me like that again. It's not the money I care about, you know that, George. It's because I grew up poor and frightened. All alone, like some orphan in the rain.

GEORGE. Well you're doing all right now. Just look at this place. It's like a fancy French chapeau. By the way, I've got that new contract with Paramount.

LILY. Oh I'm so glad you mentioned that. I want it changed. I want eighty thousand dollars for the next picture. Fifty is ridiculous.

GEORGE. But you signed it already.

LILY. I don't care what I signed. You're not just my lover, you're my agent now, so fix it. If they say no, let them go to hell. My public wants me back on Broadway anyhow.

GEORGE. "Broadway." That's peanuts. Forget about acting. You're a star. I know what's good for my little girl.

LILY. *(To her lover now, all peaches and cream.)* Oh, George, when I'm in New York I'll miss you terribly.

GEORGE. Lily –

LILY. One last kiss before you go, my darling. I'll be dreaming about your arms holding me every night, your little head on the pillow.

GEORGE. Lily, you don't have to dream. I'm staying on the train.

LILY. *(Out of her mood in a flash.)* What?

GEORGE. I'm staying.

LILY. What are you talking about?

GEORGE. I've decided to come with you.

LILY. George, you'll do as I tell you and get off right now.

GEORGE. And leave you alone in New York with all those men? Not a chance.

(He takes his overcoat off and throws it on a seat. The train starts.)

LILY. George! Oh, George, we're moving! *(She grabs his coat and tries to push him out the door.)* Get off, quick!

GEORGE. No!

LILY. Jump! Jump! Just do as I tell you!

GEORGE. Look! It's too late. The doors'll be locked.

LILY. Then jump out the window! *(Witheringly)* Oh, this is

fine, this is. You seem to forget entirely that I'm paying you ten percent of my earnings. As if I needed an agent. Thousands of dollars for doing absolutely nothing. And you take them, you worm!

GEORGE. Go on. Keep it up. I like seeing your true colors.

LILY. *(Trying to melt him.)* Oh, George, please. I can't stand fighting. You can still get off at the next stop. For me, darling …?

GEORGE. Lily, you're cooling off. I can tell.

LILY. That's not true! Darling. I adore you. I have nothing in the world but you. What else is there? Fame? Success? Empty words. Empty gestures.

GEORGE. Would you stop acting.

LILY. I beg your pardon?

GEORGE. I can always tell when you're acting. You repeat things. "Empty words, empty gestures." "Those baubles, those symbols." It sets up a kind of rhythm.

LILY. How dare you second guess me! How dare you!

GEORGE. See what I mean? "How dare you, how dare you –"

LILY. Ahhh!

(At this moment, the door opens, and O'MALLEY enters.)

O'MALLEY. Hello, you peculiar witch. How's the Baby Bernhardt?

(LILY instantly brightens up. Whenever she's around JAFFE and his crew, she's a whole new woman.)

LILY. Well, son of a gun. The foul Corsican himself. Who let you on this train?

O'MALLEY. Do you know all the trouble you've caused around this gondola the last half hour? We've torn it to shreds.

LILY. Who's we?

O'MALLEY. Guess.

LILY. My God! Is Oscar on the train?

O'MALLEY. The little corporal is returning from Moscow. His head bloodied, but still unbowed.

GEORGE. Jaffe's here? Oscar Jaffe? I should have guessed it. That's why you wanted me to get off this train. So you could cuddle up together.

LILY. Oh, don't be an ass. I had no idea he was on the train.

GEORGE. Are you going to see him? Huh? Tell me the truth.

LILY. See him? Do you think I'm out of my mind?! *(To O'MALLEY.)* Thank God you told me. I'm not stepping out of this room till we get to New York, I swear to God, I swear to God! That man belittled me and tortured me for six years. He ran around telling everybody "Where would Lily Garland be without the great Oscar Jaffe." Well, I think I showed him. Right to the top of the ladder, kid – and going up. Ha!

WEBB. Ha! Hiya, Lily.

(IDA has appeared in the doorway and now joins them. LILY is delighted to see her.)

LILY. Ida! You too, huh?

WEBB. Are you coming back into the fold?

GEORGE. *(Outraged)* Is she what?

WEBB. Coming back.

O'MALLEY. Two words. Rhymes with "slumming hack."

GEORGE. Oh, yeah? Well so does..."humming sack!"...

(The others look at each other and shake their heads.)

LILY. Did Jaffe tell you to come in here?!

WEBB. Now, don't fly off the handle, Lily. Confidentially, I'm not with Jaffe any more. I just wanted to tip you off to something. *(She's in front of GEORGE now and rubs the sides of his arms and feels his muscles.)* Ooh. Can we talk in front of Einstein here?

GEORGE. Listen, you can get the hell out of here. That's what you can do.

LILY. George, behave yourself and be quiet.

WEBB. Lily, I want you to listen a second. Oscar's broke. They're taking his theatre away from him.

LILY. Really?

WEBB. They've got him over a barrel with his pants down.

O'MALLEY. That's quite an image.

WEBB. I'm afraid he's going to do the Dutch act.

(She pantomimes a gun at her temple, and clicks with her tongue to indicate the shot.)

GEORGE. Kill himself?

O'MALLEY. No, point his finger at his head and click his tongue.

LILY. Is he doing that again? You know, committing suicide is an old habit of his.

WEBB. Remember the night he was going to hang himself and you stayed up all night and talked him out of it?

LILY. Well, we all make mistakes.

WEBB. It's serious, Lily. Unless you come to his rescue, it's curtains for him. You're his last chance.

LILY. Ida, I would rather drop dead where I'm standing than ever do another play for him. Now go back and tell that fake Svengali that I wouldn't wipe my feet on him if he was starving.

And I hope to God he is!

GEORGE. And she means every word of that. There wasn't single double repeat in the whole speech.

LILY. Oh George shut up.

WEBB. Lily, you can't turn your back on him. He made you!

LILY. He what?

WEBB. You know it's true. You were begging for a job. He taught you how to walk and talk and -

LILY. Get out of here! George, throw them out!

GEORGE. Gladly!

O'MALLEY. Watch it, you!

WEBB. I thought you were a bigger woman than this, Lily. I see that I was deeply mistaken.

LILY. Get out, get out, get out! *(WEBB and O'MALLEY exit. Hysterical:)* Why do they do this to me? What do they think I'm made of? Iron? Hammering and hammering at me, wherever I go. All of them, tearing at my nerves. All I want is a little peace! Oh my God, I'm having a breakdown! I'm all hot! I can feel it coming on! I won't be good for anything, and you'll all starve! You'll all starve!

GEORGE. Lily … Lily, calm down! Now listen to me. I want the simple, honest truth about you and Jaffe. Has he ever been your lover?

LILY. My lover?

GEORGE. Have you ever had sex with him.

LILY. I know what lover means, you idiot! *(With dignity:)* George, on my mother's grave, Oscar Jaffe has never laid a finger on me.

GEORGE. … I don't believe you.

LILY. Oh, George, why must you aggravate me?

GEORGE. Because I hate it when you're with other men. It

makes me nuts.

LILY. Oh, I don't know what I see in you! Either you bore me to death or you're so jealous you drive me crazy.

GEORGE. In other words, you don't love me at all. I'm nothing to you but a-a rag doll you can drag around! A piece of paper you can tear up! A flag pole you can sit on!

LILY. Oh, my precious. Forgive me. Please forgive me, I adore you so much …

GEORGE. Then tell me the truth about Jaffe. Please.

LILY. It is the truth. I've told you about all my lovers, every one of them. The Chinese acrobat who tried doing everything upside-down. He almost killed me. The little Philippino monk with the black hood and the candles. Even the Italian midget with the huge hands. Oh, the midget was hard to confess. And now you think I'm just a wanton. A country wench. Oh, forgive me. Please, darling, don't look down on me.

GEORGE. Look down on you? Oh, Lily, your honesty is the only thing that's saved our love. This will be the last time I'll ever ask. I promise. Did Jaffe ever touch you as a woman?

LILY. *(With great conviction.)* Never. I swear to God.

(They fall into each other's arms, and GEORGE covers her with kisses.)

GEORGE. Oh, thank God, thank God, thank God …

(Drawing Room A, JAFFE and O'MALLEY enter.)

JAFFE. The first time I slept with Lily Garland was the greatest night of my life. I remember it like it was yesterday, Owen. Now what did she say? Tell me everything.

O'MALLEY. You know her. She screamed like a fish wife.

JAFFE. Good sign. It shows the battery isn't dead. You didn't make her feel necessary, did you?

O'MALLEY. Not a word.

JAFFE. Good. Ha, ha. Now for a little surprise. I'm going to sweep her off her feet.

(He glances in a mirror, musses his hair just right and pulls open the connecting door.
Lights up in B.
JAFFE sees LILY and GEORGE in their clinch, nuzzling and kissing with great abandon. They don't see JAFFE.)

LILY. Oh, my darling, my darling …

GEORGE. You're so beautiful … so gentle …

(JAFFE closes the door and reels backward. The room is spinning.)

JAFFE. My God … Did you hear that …? Who's that man?

O'MALLEY. That's her agent. I think he's negotiating.

JAFFE. Can you believe it?! That trollop! That baggage! Mousing around with boys after what she's had. I always knew she'd head for the gutter! Get me Ida right away.

O'MALLEY. You want her back?

JAFFE. Get her back this instant! *(Through the door.)* IDAAAAAAAAAAAAAAA!!

(The train whistle blows, and the sound of it merges with OSCAR'S scream.
The action shifts to the Observation Car. The CONDUCTOR is reading a telegram while the PORTER looks on.)

CONDUCTOR. Oh my God. I wouldn't have believed it.

PORTER. What?

CONDUCTOR. The fellow that's been putting them stickers up. It's Mr. Clark, the little guy in room D. This telegram's from his nephew. It says that Clark escaped from an asylum. He's a religious nut and does this all the time. Used to be president of some big company. *(Reading)* "Will pick him up at Toledo. Accept no checks."

PORTER. I just saw him walking out toward the dining car.

CONDUCTOR. Come on. We'll take him into custody.

PORTER. Wait! There he is! He's coming this way.

CONDUCTOR. All right, all right. Keep cool. Nice and quiet. He may be dangerous ...

(CLARK enters.)

CONDUCTOR. *(Quietly)* Is your name Matthew Clark?

CLARK. *(Meekly)* Yes, sir.

(They pounce with a bang.)

CONDUCTOR. All right, Jimmy. Grab him!

PORTER. I got him! I got him!

CLARK. Please ... please! This isn't necessary.

CONDUCTOR. Oh, it isn't, huh? Then what's the idea of pasting up all those stickers?

CLARK. Oh, dear. I'm so ashamed of myself.

CONDUCTOR. You nearly caused a panic among the passegers. "The Time is at and."

PORTER. We were worried about a wreck!

CLARK. Oh, no, that's awful.

CONDUCTOR. Why do you do it?

CLARK. Well, I feel so strongly about the spiritual aspect of our lives and I get this urge to save people. Sometimes it's over-whelming.

CONDUCTOR. *(Concerned)* How do you feel now?

CLARK. I'm perfectly normal, now, I assure you.

CONDUCTOR. We got a wire here from your nephew, says you escaped out of some asylum.

CLARK. A sanitarium, sir. For some rest. And it was very wrong of me. But you see there's a convention in New York for the pharmaceutical people. That's my line. *(He pulls out a card.)* "Laxo Fruit Tablets. They keep you moving."

PORTER. They sure do.

CLARK. I'm the President of the company. And please, let me pay for what I've done.

CONDUCTOR. We don't want your money, sir. I'm sorry you've got this problem, though.

CLARK. Thank you very much. You can trust me. It's over now. Here's the rest of the stickers.

(He hands his satchel to the CONDUCTOR.)

CONDUCTOR. Thanks. You'd better go back to your room now, Mr. Clark. We'll see that you're taken care of.

CLARK. Thank you, sir. You are good people. I only wish I could feed you on loaves and fishes. Conductor.

(CLARK walks out – and the CONDUCTOR and PORTER look at each other uneasily.
The action shifts to Drawing Room A. JAFFE and WEBB.)

JAFFE. Take out your pencil, Ida. We're going to draw up a

contract between Oscar Jaffe and Lily Garland. Incidentally, I want you to know that I took you back on account of your aging mother.

WEBB. She's dead.

JAFFE. Your father, then. There's no need making the innocent suffer.

WEBB. Thanks, Oscar.

JAFFE. Draw up the contract in legal form. We'll get her a car to go to and from the theatre. Catering on matinee days.

WEBB. Oscar, at the risk of losing my job again, I have to tell you – I think this is getting us nowhere. What we need is a play. She won't sign a contract until we have one. Something she can read.

JAFFE. Oh, I'll find a play.

WEBB. Where? That's the trouble. You of all people know that you can't just pull a play out of a hat. Not a real play.

JAFFE. *(Drawing an imaginary bow and beaming.)* I was born under the sign of Sagittarius. That's the archer. It means I find things. Draw up the contract, Ida.

(The buzzer sounds.)

WEBB. Come in!

(The door opens and the BEARD appears. He's a strange, foreign-looking gentleman with a luxuriant beard. He has a heavy German accent.)

BEARD. Exgoose me, plis … *(He sees JAFFE.)* Maestro! Maestro! Iss you. I recognize you from der pictures!

(He reverently kisses JAFFE's hand.)

WEBB. Run along, we're busy!

BEARD. You are genius! You are greatest theatre-man in vorld! I k-neel at your feets!

JAFFE. Let him stay, Ida. I turn away no one. What is it you wish, my son?

BEARD. Herr Maestro, diss iss grade, grade honor. My friends in der back of train vill be so chelous. But maybe you have seen us somedime. Ja? On der stage?

WEBB. Oh, not actors!

BEARD. Ja, Ja. Actors. Ve are pelonging to der Passion Play. In Chermany.

JAFFE. Oh my God, of course! The Oberammergau Players! I should have recognized you. They're an institution, Ida. The purest branch of theatre in the world. They've been putting on the Passion Play every year for centuries.

BEARD. Ja, ja!

WEBB. Glad to meet you.

JAFFE. They are the only true actors we have left. Not like our cheap Broadway hams. These people are consecrated to their art from infancy. For hundreds of years they have made the name of Oberammergau famous. It must have started in ...

BEARD. Sixdeen hundred und thirdy-three.

JAFFE. What part do you play?

BEARD. I am der Christus.

JAFFE. Sir, I'm honored. ...

(JAFFE stops cold. He looks Heavenward and stops breathing. He gets a faraway look in his eyes. The BEARD and WEBB look at each other in perplexity.)

JAFFE. Wait!

BEARD. Vhat …?

WEBB. Oscar – ?

JAFFE. Be quiet! *(Another pause. He's thinking like mad. His eyes glow like hot coals.)* I've got it.

WEBB. Got what?

JAFFE. *(To the BEARD, brimming with mystery and purpose.)* Sit down, sir. Please, sit down. *(Softly, to himself:)* It's an inspiration! At the eleventh hour. With my back against the wall.

WEBB. What the hell are you talking about?!

JAFFE. The Passion Play! The greatest drama in the world! With Lily Garland as the Magdalene. It's perfect. Oh, my God. At last I've got something worthy of me. Sign him up. Wait. Is the whole troupe on board?

BEARD. Ja. Ve got all ten.

JAFFE. Sign them up immediately.

WEBB. May I see you alone, Oscar?

JAFFE. Not now.

WEBB. Just for a minute. *(To the BEARD, leading him to the door.)* I'm sorry, could you leave us now?

JAFFE. Ida, stop it. Are you crazy?

WEBB. *(Starting to lose control of himself.)* Never mind who's crazy.

JAFFE. Ida, what are you doing?!

(JAFFE grabs WEBB and holds him back. They struggle.)

WEBB. Oscar, you can't sign him up! I won't let you!

JAFFE. Ida -! This man is an artist! Apologize this instant!

WEBB. *(Pleading)* Oscar, please! You may not think so, but I'm more than just your manager. I'm your best friend on earth and this is crazy! You'll lose everything! Oscar, please!

(She starts to cry. JAFFE lays a hand on her shoulder.)

JAFFE. Easy, old girl. *(To the BEARD.)* She gets emotional.

WEBB. I'm not going to let you get mixed up again with a lot of phony art!

JAFFE. The trouble with you, Ida, is you don't know what's happened to the theatre public in the last few years. Well, I'll tell you. I've had my ear to the ground – like an Indian. *(Mysteriously exalted.)* People are tired of the same old thing. Humdrum, pedestrian lives played out in boring little rooms. Either it's constipated English people sipping gin and tonic through their overbites, or a bunch of hillbilly farmers crying to each other about their stinking crops, or it's little alcoholic Irish people having fights and being adorable. But I'm going to give them something colossal. Something new and magnificent. It will make history. Something that has never been done in this country before. I can see it now, in lights over Times Square. "Oberammergau on Broadway!"

(We hear the loud horn and rushing wheels of a passing train as the action shifts to:
The Observation Car. CLARK and the CONDUCTOR are just entering.)

CONDUCTOR. I don't know about this. I'd rather you stayed in your room.

CLARK. Honestly, Conductor, I'm quite all right. You see, I've been in my room studying the Bible. But the print is too small in this light, so I thought I'd see if you had a magazine.

CONDUCTOR. Yes, sir – here's one right here. Why don't you take it back to your room.

CLARK. Thank you, sir. I'll just sit here, if you don't mind.

CONDUCTOR. Well, I guess. But if you start feeling funny, just call me.

CLARK. I will, thank you.

(As the CONDUCTOR exits, LOCKWOOD and ANITA enter.)

ANITA. Grover, how could you demean yourself and even talk to the man!

DR. LOCKWOOD. He's a famous producer! It was a chance in a million! Look. Look who's coming.

(O'MALLEY enters.)

ANITA. Oh, no ...

DR. LOCKWOOD. Hi. How are you?

O'MALLEY. If it ain't Shakespeare himself. And Annie Hathaway.

DR. LOCKWOOD. Has Mr. Jaffe read my play yet?

O'MALLEY. I think he has, now that you mention it.

DR. LOCKWOOD. *(Excited)* Really?! What does he think?! Does he like it?!

O'MALLEY. He hasn't told me yet, but I know he's always wanted to produce two plays in a row about Joan of Arc.

DR. LOCKWOOD. Oh my God! I feel so close! Listen. Do me a favor. I know this sounds a bit unorthodox, but tell him that if he does the play on Broadway, I'll throw in free surgery for the whole cast. I do gall bladders, prostates ...

O'MALLEY. Well now, that could just make all the difference.

DR. LOCKWOOD. Oh Anita, I feel inspired. Come on! I'm

going to write a whole new play tonight! About theatre people like Mr. O'Malley and Mr. Jaffe – generous, big-hearted troopers who give people like me a chance.

ANITA. And what happens after the dream sequence?

(LOCKWOOD hurries out. ANITA starts to follow, but O'MALLEY blocks her way – then kisses her, bending her back – a really great kiss. She pulls away and looks furious ... then grabs him and kisses him back and exits. He starts to go out after her, when IDA enters from the same direction and stops him.)

WEBB. Owen! Now listen. I've got a message from the Earth-shaker. He wants you to find him a Bible.

(CLARK hears the word Bible and reacts.)

O'MALLEY. A Bible? Now where am I supposed to find a Bible on this big jalopy.

WEBB. I have no idea, but he says it's life and death.

O'MALLEY. "Life and death." He'd say that about a ham sandwich if he was hungry. I'll do some looking.

(O'MALLEY exits. WEBB sits down next to CLARK and takes a breath. CLARK reads his magazine. Then:)

CLARK. *(Indicating the Saturday Evening Post that he's reading.)* Good magazine.

WEBB. Yes, it is.

CLARK. I'm one of their biggest advertisers.

WEBB. No kidding.

CLARK. Of course, I'd prefer the newspapers, if I could reconcile my conscience to Sunday advertising.

WEBB. What's your line?

CLARK. Household remedies and pharmaceuticals. *(He pulls out a business card.)* "Laxo Fruit Tablets. They Keep You Moving." I'm the President.

WEBB. *(Impressed)* Well isn't that something. I don't suppose the remedy business was hit much by the depression.

CLARK. No, no, no, no, no. We've been sailing right along. In fact, profits have doubled.

WEBB. No kidding.

CLARK. My company is so glutted with cash at the moment that I'm looking for something to invest in. Do you have any ideas?

(Beat. WEBB's eyes light up like sparklers.)

WEBB. Well, have you ever thought of investing in the theatre?

CLARK. The theatre?

WEBB. Yes, no one ever loses any money in the theatre.

(They walk off together – and the action shifts to:
Drawing Room A. JAFFE is pacing impatiently, when O'MALLEY enters.)

O'MALLEY. There ain't a Bible this side of Buffalo.

JAFFE. Well keep looking. I need to plunder a copy for extra scenes. However, we can't delay. The troops are lining up before Waterloo.

O'MALLEY. What's the program, Napoleon?

(JAFFE holds up a large silk bandana, which he begins to fashion into a sling.)

JAFFE. Step one: eliminate the lover. Tie this in back.

O'MALLEY. How did you hurt your wing?

JAFFE. I didn't. It's a little strategy in case the young ruffian in there turns violent. He'd never hit a wounded man. How do I look?

O'MALLEY. Wounded.

JAFFE. Good. Hold the fort. I've got to go break a human heart. Ha ha!

(JAFFE clutches an imaginary heart in his free hand, and opens the connecting door. Lights up in B. LILY and GEORGE are curled up on a chair together in a romantic embrace.)

LILY. I've always wanted a real house, with a garden. And a cookie jar. And a roof. Oh God, it's you.

GEORGE. Jaffe!

JAFFE. *(His voice ineffably tender.)* Hello, Lily. I heard you were on the train, so I dropped in to say hello.

LILY. Please go, Oscar. I have nothing to say to you.

JAFFE. May I at least meet your friend? How young he looks. Are you adopting him?

LILY. George, this is Oscar Jaffe, Worm Extraordinaire.

(GEORGE laughs.)

JAFFE. I wouldn't snigger if I were you. She'll be calling you names in no time.

GEORGE. *(Aggressively)* Listen, Jaffe, I'm warning you right now. Don't bother Miss Garland, and I mean it.

LILY. No violence, George.

GEORGE. *(Advancing on JAFFE.)* I want him to get out!

JAFFE. *(Holding his crippled arm in front of him like a shield.)* My arm! Be careful! It's broken!

GEORGE. Good, I'll break the other one!

JAFFE. *(To LILY.)* I can see why you like him. He's rather pre-historic. Like one of those huge green dinosaurs with the very small heads.

GEORGE. *(Attacking JAFFE.)* You take that back!

JAFFE. My arm! My arm!

LILY. Stop it! Stop it both of you! *(GEORGE backs off.)* Oh, that would really finish me. A public fight. *(To JAFFE.)* You'd like nothing better than flashing our names on the front pages.

JAFFE. *(Speaks out of heartbreak.)* Let him throw me out, Lily. It would be the final irony. I welcome it.

GEORGE. Good, then get out! You have no rights in here.

JAFFE. No rights? He doesn't know about us?

LILY. *(Panicky)* Shut up, Oscar, and leave.

JAFFE. No, I must explain my position to this young man. *(He turns to GEORGE.)* You see, Lily and I were lovers once. It was, I confess, one of the great romances of all time. George, you should have seen her in bed.

GEORGE. Oh my God …

JAFFE. She was remarkable! Inventive, athletic –

GEORGE. I don't want to hear it!

JAFFE. As though she were trained in a circus –

LILY. Oscar, stop it!! Oh, you could never stand to see anything sweet and decent in my life. You had to come in here and blab.

JAFFE. *(Wounded)* Blab! Is that what you call it? I'm proud of every hour we spent together.

GEORGE. *(To LILY.)* So you were lying to me. Right to my face. With every breath.

LILY. Don't start hammering at me. Hammering and hammering! I can't stand it. Oh, my God!

(She bursts into tears and sobs.)

JAFFE. Comfort her, sir. That is your privilege.

LILY. *(To GEORGE through her racking sobs.)* I tried to save you the pain. Yes, I lied! But only to save you ...

JAFFE. That's from "Sappho."

LILY. Get out!

GEORGE. Lily, how could you?!

LILY. Darling, I hate him! He means nothing to me! The dirt under my feet! George – darling, look at me ...!

(She breaks down. GEORGE pulls his hand away, turns on his heel and walks out of the room, chin high, without saying a word.)

JAFFE. What an exit! Not a word! That's the exit we should have had in "Gypsy Heart" in the second act.

LILY. Oh, go and crawl back under your stone, or wherever you came from. There's nothing left for me to do but kill myself. Nothing left at all.

JAFFE. *(Happily)* I wouldn't do it yet. I've got a wonderful surprise for you. Don't go away, I'll be right back.

(JAFFE skips back into A, where O'MALLEY is waiting for him. He pulls off the scarf and tosses it aside.)

JAFFE. Owen, I've just played a scene that Puccini might have written for La Bohème. Now where's Ida with that contract? I need the contract! I've got Lilly in the perfect mood and it's time to strike. Come on. Quickly!

(He and O'MALLEY hurry out the door to the corridor.
Meanwhile, in B, LILY has sunk dejectedly into a chair. After a
*   beat, GEORGE enters. For a moment, he just looks at her,*
*   square-jawed. Then:)*

GEORGE. Are you still in love with him?

LILY. I hate him. And I hate you. I despise all men.

GEORGE. Were you really lovers?

LILY. Of course we were, you idiot. I starred in eight of his productions. We shared a house together. What do you think we did at night, play Mahjongg?

GEORGE. *(Savagely)* Then why did you lie to me? Swearing on your love and honor. What a fake you are!

LILY. I'm a fake?! Me?! *(She laughs hysterically.)* You've been catting around Hollywood since the day you arrived. But you're a man and I'm a woman. So I'm supposed to be chaste and pure? Do you want to know something? I never told you the truth in my life. I lied about all of them!

GEORGE. There was no midget?

LILY. There were two midgets! And the acrobat had a horse!!

GEORGE. My God! And you wanted my respect!

LILY. Oh, who cares about your respect. I'm too big to be respected. The men I've known have understood that.

GEORGE. Men you've known! Like Jaffe, you mean!

LILY. Yes, Jaffe. He'll tell you what I am: a first class passenger entitled to privileges.

GEORGE. *(Sarcastically)* Oh, you're an artist.

LILY. You're God damn right I am.

GEORGE. You're no woman. You're like some kind of pet monkey full of tricks and vanities.

LILY. Oh shut up, George. You bore me to death.

GEORGE. I came in to forgive you. To give you another chance. But I'll see you damned before I ever speak to you again.

LILY. My last two words to you are: I hate you. I despise you. Now get out of my life. I throw you away. *(GEORGE exits to the corridor, slamming the door. LILY is alone.)* Oh, God, I'm so sick of myself.

(Drawing Room A. JAFFE bursts in, followed by O'MALLEY.)

JAFFE. When I find Ida, I'm going to wring her neck. I need that contract!

O'MALLEY. I don't know where else to look. She must be hiding in some compartment.

JAFFE. Go look again. Start at the engine and work back. Did you find the Bible yet?

O'MALLEY. Not yet.

JAFFE. Well find that too. Now get going!

O'MALLEY. Yes, sir!

(O'MALLEY exits.

JAFFE takes a breath. He thinks. He walks to the connecting door, puts his ear to it and listens. He hears nothing. He straightens his robe, musses his hair, then opens the door and goes in. LILY looks up.)

LILY. What do you want? Scorpion.

JAFFE. If it makes you happier to call me names, go ahead. Please.

LILY. Oscar, you're the most horrible excuse for a human being that ever walked on two legs.

JAFFE. Is this about your friend George? Because if he'd

been a real man, he would have taken you in his arms. It was a chance to show his love and what did he do? Walked out with the clenched look of a Puritan with diarrhea.

LILY. Your philosophy of love doesn't interest me, Mr. Jaffe.

JAFFE. I'm an Oriental, Lily. My love for you blinded me. That was always the trouble between us as producer and artist.

LILY. Oh, that's what it was, was it? How about your name in electric lights bigger than everybody else's? Your grand delusions that you were Shakespeare, Cardinal Richelieu and the Grand Lama of Tibet all rolled into one?

JAFFE. You're right.

LILY. I am?

JAFFE. I admit it. We do get wiser as we get older. I never appreciated your real greatness until I lost you. That last argument we had about percentages – God! How small and cheap I was!

LILY. Remember those quotes you gave the papers when I threatened to leave? "Miss Garland is progressing nicely. Of course, I taught her everything she knows. It was like training an old cocker spaniel who thinks very slowly."

(They both laugh. It's real this time. For the first time since we've met them, they seem relaxed and at ease with each other. Obviously, they love each other's company.)

JAFFE. God, I was despicable!

(He takes off the sling.)

LILY. I knew it!

JAFFE. And I knew you knew it. I can't believe I let you get away.

LILY. We let each other get away.

JAFFE. We had so much going for us. Looks. Money. Fame. Or maybe that was the problem. Maybe we'd have been all right together if we'd lived on a farm somewhere and grown potatoes.

LIL. I could have worn a polka-dot dress and slapped the hogs.

JAFFE. "Slopped" the hogs.

LILY. Right. I could have scrubbed the South Forty, then milked the steers.

JAFFE. You were never much of a country girl, were you.

LILY. We should have tried it, though. We might not have argued as much.

JAFFE. We never really argued.

LILY. Oh, please. Do you remember that time I played Hedda Gabler? I took an ax off the wall and tried to attack you in the wings. Then I chased you down 45th Street.

JAFFE. Or that time I broke your finger.

LILY. That was an accident. You were putting up a picture and I was holding the nail. The hammer slipped.

JAFFE. No it didn't. It was deliberate. I was angry at you for the night before.

LILY. What happened the night before?

JAFFE. We were at the Roosevelt party. You wouldn't dance with me.

LILY. Because you slept with that woman when you thought I wasn't looking. What was her name. Teddy's cousin. … Eleanor.

JAFFE. I wonder what happened to her …?

LILY. We don't know anything about love, do we? Unless it's written and rehearsed. We're only real between curtains.

JAFFE. I could cut my throat for losing you.

LILY. If you did, grease paint would run out of it.

JAFFE. I've paid for it, a thousand times. When I saw that

movie of yours …

LILY. *(Quickly, interested.)* Did you like it?

JAFFE. I wanted to vomit. All your talent wasted, Lily.

LILY. *(Defensively)* Well, you'll be interested to know that it's a great success. The critics said I was marvelous in it. Superb. Here, if you don't believe me, look.

(She hands him her Academy Award.)

JAFFE. What's this?

LILY. It's an Academy Award. They're thinking of calling it the "Oscar."

OSCAR. God forbid.

LILY. *(With quiet triumph.)* Read what it says.

JAFFE. "The Academy of Motion Picture Arts and Science." "Best Actress." Good God! It's pathetic. Don't fall for this sort of thing, Lily. You deserve better. God, the direction of that movie, it was despicable. And the lighting – ! Don't you remember how I always brought the lights up every time you stepped on stage? You became radiant. People left the theatre feeling spiritual.

LILY. Listen, Oscar, if all this adagio is preliminary to a contract offer, you can save your breath.

JAFFE. *(Indignant)* Who said anything about contracts? Shame on you, Lily!

LILY. Oscar, you'd do anything to get my name on a contract and you know it. But I can't blame you, I do sell a lot of tickets.

JAFFE. *(Witheringly)* That statue must have done this to you. I haven't come here with any contracts. I'm not Max Jacobs. I came in here with a dream, a dream we both had long ago. The part we planned as a climax to your career. The last golden stair … *(An awed whisper.)* The great courtesan role.

LILY. Oh, my God! So that's the big surprise you have for me. Another role where I make the great sacrifice, offer my broken body to the villain for my brother's life.

JAFFE. You didn't do badly with Anna Christie. Or Roxane. Or Cleopatra. And now I'm talking about the greatest woman of all time. Just her memory has kept the world weeping for centuries. *(Train whistle. He seizes upon it as an orchestral accompaniment.)* The Magdalene! *(She doesn't get it.)* Mary Magdalene. The wanton prostitute saved by Jesus Christ himself. The fallen woman whom he rescues from a life of filth and who must then witness his heartbreaking crucifixion at the hands of their enemies.

LILY. Who wrote it?

JAFFE. God wrote it.

LILY. I mean who wrote the play!

JAFFE. No one knows. It's been done for centuries in the little town of Oberammergau. You see, I'm going to put the Passion Play on in New York. I've had it up my sleeve for years, waiting for the right moment. The wickedest woman of her age – sensual, heartless and beautiful. Corrupting everything she touches, running the gamut from the gutter to glory! Can you see her, Lily … this little wanton, ending up in tears at the foot of the Cross. Wait! I have an idea! I'll have Judas strangle himself with her hair.

LILY. No, no, no – wait! Why not have Judas drink the poison that was intended for Mary.

JAFFE. That's an inspiration!

LILY. Then he dies in agony as she stands over him and watches. "Die! Die! Die, thou wicked creature!"

JAFFE. Lily, that's it! You have it! I see the whole thing. I see the Magdalene as a fine, aristocratic woman with folds of silk framing her forehead. Then, after being heartbroken by someone she loves, she goes down, down into the depths … I'm going to make it my greatest production ever. I've brought over an entire troupe from Europe – I flew to Nuremberg to find them. Lily, I've run the figures. If the play runs for five years I won't make a cent. You can have all the money. I only want to stagger New York. I want a desert scene with real camels and sand from the Holy Land. *(He starts pacing.)* I'll have a banquet that you give for your lover in the Second Act. Pontius Pilate, Governor of Judea. You have your slaves all around you, and you're covered in emeralds from head to foot without a stitch of clothing underneath. "Pontius, why do you stare at me. Have you not seen my gems before?" Your skin is like porcelain, almost transparent in its fineness – think of Michelangelo, the Pièta. Pilate begs you to marry him and you laugh in his face, haha!, despising all men for what they did to you. Your cruel, terrible laughter rings through the palace and makes his blood run cold. "My blood, it's cold." But that's nothing compared to the finish, where you stand in rags in the anteroom and the Emperor Nero himself offers you half his empire. You answer him with a speech that may be the greatest piece of literature ever written, with the sun pouring down on you, transfigured with love and sacrifice! "Never!" you cry. "Never will I betray the love and trust of he who loves and trusts us all!" Nero cringes! – you push him away! – "Ha!" – and the last we see of you, as the curtain falls, is this pathetic little figure in the distance, selling olives in the market place. "Olives ... olives ... Three for a drachma ... Olives ..." *(He bows his head in conclusion. Pause. Then LILY bursts into a loud laugh.)* What is it?

LILY. Oscar, you are a pure case of leaping insanity. You must have been dropped on your head as a child.

JAFFE. Lily!

LILY. Coming in here with real camels, and sand from the Holy Land. You're a scream! You're going to put on the Passion

Play?! You haven't a hundred dollars to your name.

JAFFE. I can raise every penny!

LILY. *(Furiously)* Yes, and I know just how you intend to raise it. Get my name on a contract and go out and peddle it. Well, no thank you. I'm through being your meal ticket.

JAFFE. *(With great dignity.)* You're at liberty to call up any one of my banks in the morning.

LILY. Your banks. Do you mean the ones that are taking your theatre away from you?

JAFFE. That's a lie! You've been listening to my enemies!

LILY. I've been listening to Miss Ida Webb, your loyal business manager, who came in here with some sob story about you committing suicide unless I took pity on you.

JAFFE. She didn't! She wouldn't!

LILY. She told me everything! She said you don't have a dime! You're broke! Busted!

JAFFE. It was revenge! I fired her for stealing!

LILY. Oh, shut up.

JAFFE. She had a private Swiss bank account under the name Eric von Stroheim!

LILY. I've had enough of your lies!

JAFFE. I'm offering you a chance to become immortal.

LILY. Thank you, but I've decided to stay mortal with a real producer.

JAFFE. Who?

LILY. He sent me the contract this morning.

JAFFE. Who is it?!

LILY. Max Jacobs. Does that ring a bell?

JAFFE. *(Stunned)* Max Jacobs?

LILY. Read the papers tomorrow morning.

JAFFE. You can't sign with him. He's a thief! A sex maniac!

LILY. Oh, Oscar –

JAFFE. I caught him in the men's room with my secretary and a small dog!

LILY. Oscar!

JAFFE. He's illiterate! He can hardly write his own name!

LILY. He writes it all right on checks. Great big checks, too.

JAFFE. Oh, it's money. That's all you want. Just another greedy ham. If I jingled a few miserable dollars at you, your mouth would begin to water and you'd start drooling and squealing "gimme, gimme, gimme …"

LILY. *(Cheerfully)* That's right, Oscar. Now, get out before I have the porter throw you off the train.

JAFFE. Look out who gets thrown off the train. Travelling with a gigolo.

LILY. Get out of here, you swindler! You fake!

(She hits him. He defends himself.)

JAFFE. Stop that, you cheap little shop girl!

LILY. *(Pummelling him.)* Get out, get out, get out!

JAFFE. I'll tell the world who's a fake. You are!

LILY. Liar!

OSCAR. I made you!

LILY. Liar!

OSCAR. I taught you everything you know!

LILY. *(Overlapping)* Liar! Liar! Liar!

JAFFE. Your voice – your walk – even your name – Lily Garland! I gave you that! Ahh!

(She's kicked him hard, and he throws her down on the seat.)

LILY. Ahh!

JAFFE. *(Standing over her, furious.)* As there is a God in heaven, you'll end up where you belong, in a burlesque house, Miss Mildred Plotka!

LILY. AHHHHHHHHH!

(He turns with the dignity of an outraged cardinal and sweeps into Drawing Room A. LILY screams with frustration.

Lights down in B and up in A. O'MALLEY is there. JAFFE slams the connecting door and stomps in.)

JAFFE. Where's Ida?! Where is that traitor Webb?! I'm going to strangle her with my bare hands, so help me God!

(The door opens and WEBB enters.)

WEBB. *(Unsuspecting)* Oscar, guess what?

JAFFE. You traitor! You miserable Mata Hari!

WEBB. Oscar, listen to me!! *(JAFFE stands back, panting; WEBB is excited.)* Do you have any idea who I've got with me outside? Matthew Clark, the patent medicine king. *(JAFFE looks puzzled.)* I've talked him into financing the Passion Play from the religious angle. You can write your own ticket. He has millions!

JAFFE. *(Hoarsely)* Where is he?

WEBB. Right outside. Shall I bring him in?

JAFFE. Yes! Yes! Hurry it up!

WEBB. Come in, Mr. Clark. *(CLARK enters.)* Matthew Clark, this is Oscar Jaffe.

JAFFE. *(The air of a cardinal again; he bows with consummate dignity.)* How do you do, sir?

CLARK. Miss Webb has told me all about you. It's so unusual to find a man of your profession so interested in religion. What is your denomination, Mr. Jaffe?

(JAFFE looks quickly towards WEBB, who forms the word "Baptist" with his lips. JAFFE tries in vain to pick it up.)

JAFFE. ... Denomination ... Of course ... My-my denomination ...*(WEBB – behind CLARK – has an inspiration. She seizes a glass of water – or a flower vase from which she snatches the flowers – and empties the water over O'MALLEY'S head. JAFFE reacts at once.)* Sir, I'm proud to say that I'm a Baptist.
CLARK. Hallelujah!
ALL. Hallelujah!

(Blackout.)

End of Act One

ACT II

Scene 1

(Train whistle before rise of curtain. Drawing Room A. JAFFE, before Austerlitz, in purple pajamas and robe, has been dictating telegrams to the CONDUCTOR who has a pad in hand. O'MALLEY is listening, bemused.)

JAFFE. I want all those telegrams on the wire the moment the train stops. The Passion Play is in production.

CONDUCTOR. I'll file them in Cleveland. Is that all?

JAFFE. No, my good man. I haven't begun yet.

CONDUCTOR. I'll have to get some more blanks.

JAFFE. Please do, and please hurry. It's a matter of life and death. *(The CONDUCTOR exits.)* Owen, how much money did I tell Mr. Clark we needed to start with?

OWEN. Three hundred thousand potatoes.

JAFFE. I should have said three hundred and fifty thousand. Go get him, Owen. He took me by surprise. It was the artist in me that spoke, not the businessman.

O'MALLEY. I wouldn't bear down on him so soon, Oscar. That's a big bag of money.

JAFFE. It seems like nothing to me. Mere confetti that I scatter in the wind like dust –

O'MALLEY. Oscar!

JAFFE. But perhaps you're right. Mr. Clark impressed me as being something of a dreamer.

O'MALLEY. He's got me baffled. He twitters away like some dithering Saint.

JAFFE. I've always attracted that kind of man. They respond to something spiritual in me. Wait! I forgot to tell Lily about the money.

(JAFFE hurries into Drawing Room B.)

JAFFE. Lily! Guess what?! I have good news! No, not just good. Spectacular news!

LILY. How dare you come in here again?

JAFFE. Oh stop it. We had a few words. So what. I accept your apology.

LILY. My apology?! Why you –

JAFFE. Would you listen to me?! The Passion Play now has a backer! Ida found him. He's the President of Clark-Reiney Pharmaceuticals and he's worth a fortune!

LILY. Oh Oscar, please …

JAFFE. It's true! He's some religious fanatic – knows the Bible forwards and backwards – and he's writing us a check as a first installment. Just to get us started.

LILY. Oscar, is this true?

JAFFE. Yes, yes, yes! I swear on my mother's grave!

LILY. Your mother's not dead.

JAFFE. That's not the point! Look. You can meet him. Mr. Clark. You can ask him yourself. You can ask him anything!

LILY. Why does this sound fishy to me, like an Oscar Jaffe Special?

JAFFE. For God's sake, woman, do you want to be in the play or not?!

LILY. Yes! Of course I do! From what you said, it could be the best thing we ever did together. But Oscar …

JAFFE. But what? What "Oscar?" What is the problem?

LILY. Oscar, you know that I would walk through fire to be in another truly great production with you.

JAFFE. Well –

LILY. That the best times of my life were being in the theatre next to you, doing something that truly mattered. But when I think how many times you made me promises you never kept. You never intended to keep.

JAFFE. How can you say that? I intended to keep every one of them. And I bent over backwards to make them happen, just for you. Medea – your finest hour. Desdemona – you were a goddess. Sacajawea was a mistake, I admit, but this time, Lily, it's a dead certainty. Now are you with me or not?! Yes or no?!

LILY. Yes! Yes! Oscar I'm with you.

JAFFE. Heart and soul?

LILY. Heart and soul.

(They embrace joyfully.)

JAFFE. Now fix yourself up. You look hideous. Repair that face and find yourself a decent dress. I want to introduce Matthew Clark to the great Lily Garland. Be alluring. Difficult. Winsome. Impossible. In other words, be yourself. Ha!

(JAFFE hurries back into Drawing Room A. The buzzer sounds and the CONDUCTOR enters.)

CONDUCTOR. I've got the blanks now.

JAFFE. Good. We'll resume. The next telegram goes to John Ringling, of the Ringling Brothers Circus. Owen, you'll have to find out the address immediately. "Dear John, I am in the market for twenty-five camels, four elephants and an ibis." That's the royal bird of Egypt. "Wire me your rock bottom price. Oscar Jaffe." He'll be a little miffed but I'm going to cable the Berlin zoo for the lions. They have the best specimens. We'll need about ten or twelve. Make a note, Owen.

O'MALLEY. Where are you going to house these monsters?

JAFFE. I'll construct a little zoo off the green room. I'm going to rebuild the entire theatre to make it resemble a grotto. Owen, do you remember the name of the Sultan of Turkey?

O'MALLEY. Not offhand. Who's he gonna play?

JAFFE. I don't want him. I want his dervishes. The whirling ones. We'll need a dozen. Remind me to take the matter up with the Turkish and Arabian consuls. How many sheep did I order?

CONDUCTOR. Uh, twenty.

JAFFE. Change that to read fifty. We don't want to stint. We must have a complete flock. Now take a wire to Ricard Strauss.

CONDUCTOR. You mean the composer?

JAFFE. No, Ricard Strauss the plumber. Yes of course the composer! The greatest of the century. He's in New York at the moment, so we're in luck. "Dear Ricard: Need you to write score for Passion Play. The one with Christ in it. Want it to sound like *"Salomé"* but not so much French horn this time. Meet me for lunch on Thursday at the Palm Court. Oscar Jaffe."

(The buzzer sounds. O'MALLEY opens the door and we see the BEARD standing there. O'MALLEY closes the door on him.)

O'MALLEY. The wooly sheep is at the gate.

JAFFE. Stop the tomfoolery, Owen, and let him in. Conductor, you may go now, but hold yourself in readiness.

CONDUCTOR. Yes, sir.

(The CONDUCTOR exits and the BEARD enters.)

BEARD. Maestro, ve have found first part of manusgript. Der second part is missing yet, but I can tell you vhat happens. Der Christus dies. Und den he floats up to heaven mitt der singing angels. In Chermany, ve use ropes und pullies.

JAFFE. Just leave me what you've got and keep looking. It's in German, I see.

BEARD. Ja, but I can translate. I speak der English lingvisticals as good as der Cherman. Maestro, you vill haf supper mit us? Ja? Ve got k-nockvurst.

JAFFE. Just run along. I'll send for you soon.

BEARD. Auf Wiedersehen

(He exits with a bow.)

JAFFE. They're going to be a sensation in New York. Pure artists.

(The buzzer sounds again and O'MALLEY opens the door and DR. LOCKWOOD is standing in the doorway.)

DR. LOCKWOOD. "Joan of Lorraine! Witch incarnate! I condemn thee and thy doctor to the flames of Hellfire –"

(SLAM! O'MALLEY slams the door in his face.)

JAFFE. Who was that?
O'MALLEY. I have no idea.
JAFFE. Owen, go get Lily and bring her in.
O'MALLEY. I'll be right back.

(O'MALLEY goes to B as WEBB enters from the corridor.)

WEBB. Mr. Clark's coming with his Bible, and a big, fat check!
JAFFE. Perfect.
O'MALLEY. *(In B, hollering into the bedroom:)* Hey! Lily, are you ready yet?!
LILY. *(Off – she screams like a fish-wife; we can only understand some of it, but it's something like this:)* Would you give me a minute you no good sonofabitch I'm moving as fast as I can so you can * □ *&%&)$#@$))*%$@!!!!

(O'MALLEY returns to A.)

O'MALLEY. She purred like a pussycat. She'll be right in.

(CLARK knocks on the door and WEBB opens it.)

JAFFE. Come in, sir. Please sit down.
CLARK. Thank you.
JAFFE. Miss Webb tells me you have a Bible you can loan me.
WEBB. *(Proudly)* He knows it by heart, practically.
JAFFE. *(Taking the Bible.)* The Bible. What can I say. There's nobody writing dialogue like this any more. *(Opening it to a ran-*

dom passage; with great feeling:) "Of the Tree of Knowledge of Good and Evil thou shalt not eat, for upon the day that thou eat of it, thou shalt die!" No wonder they call him God.

O'MALLEY. *(To CLARK.)* Lily will be along in a jiffy.

CLARK. Who is Lily?

JAFFE. Lily Garland – an actress I'm considering for one of the parts.

CLARK. Is she a professional actress?

JAFFE. Of course.

CLARK. Oh, I don't think that will do. I wouldn't like to have the Passion Play contaminated by any women like that.

JAFFE. Nor would I, Mr. Clark.The religious flavor must come over in a bath of glory. But I don't have to remind you the kind of woman the Magdalene was.

CLARK. Oh. Are we going to have the Magdalene in the play? She's not one of my favorite characters.

JAFFE. Nor mine. Of course. But the moment you see Miss Garland you'll realize at once that the part of the Magdalene might have been written for her. It's an opportunity we cannot cast aside lightly.

(The buzzer sounds.)

O'MALLEY. Thar she blows.

(He opens the door and LILY stands framed in the doorway, dressed to the nines in a slinky dress, her neck and wrists glittering with diamonds.)

WEBB. Hello, Lily. Welcome.

JAFFE. Dear lovely Lily.

LILY. I'm afraid you caught me quite unawares. I haven't even had a moment to change.

JAFFE. No matter, Lily. You turn this wretched little room into a palace. Allow me, the great Miss Garland, Mr. Matthew Clark.

LILY. *(Purring)* How do you do, sir? It's a great pleasure.

CLARK. *(Nervously eyeing his first harlot.)* Won't you sit down, my child?

LILY. Thank you. I just came for a moment.

WEBB. I guess you know who this is, Lily – the Clark-Reiney people. Biggest pill manufacturers in the world.

JAFFE. Shall I ring for some ginger ale, my dear? *(To CLARK.)* None of us ever touch anything in the way of liquor. It's against the rules of my organization.

(JAFFE. looks at O'MALLEY, who drops his head. Or perhaps he drops his flask.)

LILY. Nothing for me. Thank you.

CLARK. You don't look at all as I expected.

LILY. Nor do you. I expected some hard-boiled old business man, and you … you have the look of an artist about you – a creative light of passion shining from your eyes. I'm overwhelmed.

CLARK. Thank you.

LILY. And now I hear that you're joining us in that humble yet valiant little effort we call the theatre.

CLARK. Well, all I'm really doing is investing some money. I've brought along the check.

WEBB. Show it to her, Oscar. Three hundred thousand dollars, Lily.

LILY. Jesus Christ!

JAFFE. Is the subject of the play, that's correct, Lily.

LILY. Of course he is. And what a man. He's my favorite character in all of fiction.

JAFFE. Well, there it is, Lily. You can count the zeros.

(Beaming, he shows her the check.)

LILY. Oh, Mr. Clark. What a beautiful gesture.

CLARK. Well, as I was saying before, that's only a starter.

LILY. *(Now entirely charming, the grand dame of culture.)* If anyone had told me an hour ago I would be sitting here like this, discussing art and culture with a man of vision like yourself, I would have pee'd myself.

JAFFE. You might want to glance over this, Lily. It's a little contract I've drawn up for you to sign. It covers the terms of our agreement.

CLARK. We'd like to have you with us very much, Miss Garland.

LILY. Thank you, my dear man. Thank you.

(She takes the contract from JAFFE.)

CLARK. May I see that agreement for a minute?

JAFFE. After Miss Garland has signed you may read it.

CLARK. Well, now, I'm pretty good at contracts, Mr. Jaffe.

JAFFE. This is not a business transaction, sir. It's an obeisance to a lovely woman and a great artist.

LILY. Thank you, Oscar. It's just like old times, isn't it.

JAFFE. Would you like to sign it now, my dear?

LILY. I think I'll just read it first. If you don't mind. I'm delighted to know you, Mr. Clark. It's a great honor.

CLARK. I hope I haven't been too boring.

LILY. Oh, no. Very fascinating, charming. I look forward to
our association. *(Waxing poetic, laying it on thick.)* And above all,
I look forward to working on a theatrical drama set in the Holy
Land, the Land of Spirit, the Land of my Youth. I grew up there,
you see, and played in the sand along the Danube. I used to ride
camels, sitting high on their divine little humps, eating figs and
dromedaries. And do you know – even as a child, when I touched
the land, I could feel the anguish of Christ himself when he looked
down bleeding from the cross and said to the Pharaoh, "Let my
people go!"

JAFFE. Goodbye, my dear.

CLARK. You have made me very happy.

LILY. And you, I.

(She exits. JAFFE turns to CLARK.)

CLARK. She seems like a very holy woman. A little con-
fused, but holy.

JAFFE. I think you made quite an impression on her.

CLARK. Oh, dear. I tried my best not to look at her below the
neck.

(The buzzer sounds.)

JAFFE. For Christ's sake, Ida! Have a sign put on that door
– "not to be disturbed". *(The BEARD enters.)* Oh, it's you. Come
in, sir.

BEARD. I am finding second part of manuscript. It vas in
other suitcase mitt towels from last hotel.

JAFFE. Thank you. Mr. Clark, I want you to meet an extraor-
dinary man. One of the greatest artists in the world. I've engaged

him and his colleagues to play in our production.

CLARK. How do you do. *(To JAFFE.)* What part is he going to play?

BEARD. Der Christus.

JAFFE. He's been playing it for twenty years. And his father before him, and his father before that.

BEARD. Und two uncles before dem, und vun cousin who had shtutter und vas not so good.

CLARK. *(Unhappily)* Well … this is quite a surprise, Mr. Jaffe, and, I assure you, an unpleasant one. I won't say anything more. Good-bye.

(CLARK heads for the door.)

WEBB. Wait. Wait! Mr. Clark, what's the matter?

CLARK. Well, the whole idea was, as I told you, Miss Webb, that if I was going to finance the Passion Play, it would be with one proviso. That I would play the part of Christ.

JAFFE. What!

(The next five lines are simultaneous:)

CLARK. Oh, yes, Mr. Jaffe.

JAFFE. It's insane. I won't have it!

WEBB. Oh, my God. I didn't think he was serious, Oscar.

CLARK. That's the whole point of everything.

BEARD. Dot's foolish! I been playing dot part for 20 years!

JAFFE. Stop! *(Referring to the BEARD.)* Ida, show him the door! And I don't want to see anyone after this except by appointment!

WEBB. Come on, let's go.

JAFFE. I'll send for you.

BEARD. For three hundred years, Mr. Chaffee!

JAFFE. Out! *(WEBB pushes the BEARD out the door. Beat.)* All right, Mr. Clark, if you want to play Christ, you've got it. You're Christ.

CLARK. I am?

JAFFE. Absolutely. We start rehearsal in six weeks. Ida, give him the address.

CLARK. Oh, good. And you needn't worry about the lines, Mr. Jaffe. I know every single word of the text. And not just my favorite passages either.

JAFFE. *(Escorting him to the door.)* Wonderful. Now I'll see you later. Thank you. Good-bye.

CLARK. Good-bye.

(JAFFE pushes him out the door and closes it.)

WEBB. Are you really going to let him play Jesus Christ?

JAFFE. The King of Kings? Don't be insane. I wouldn't let him play King Kong. The trouble is, I don't trust him. He could change his mind in a second. I want you to hop off the train at Toledo and get this check cashed. It's on a Toledo bank.

WEBB. The National Exchange. I know the president there.

JAFFE. Splendid. I'll endorse it.

(He endorses the check.)

WEBB. I don't care to crow, Oscar, but I would like to point out that Ida Webb delivers in a pinch.

JAFFE. I've been thinking of promoting you, Ida. Remind me when we arrive in New York to get you a secretary. One that you can boss around all by yourself. Here – put this in your purse. Now where's that Bible ...? Ah. Good. *(He opens the Bible and starts to read it.)* Where's my pencil. I'm going to do a little editing.

(WEBB leaves.

The Observation Car. Discovered are ANITA, LOCKWOOD and the CONDUCTOR. ANITA is upset and tearful, and the CONDUCTOR is trying to deal with this latest crisis.)

ANITA. It's outrageous, that's what it is! Outrageous!
DR. LOCKWOOD. It isn't the conductor's fault, my dear.
CONDUCTOR. Tell me exactly what happened.
ANITA. Well, we were in the upper berth –
DR. LOCKWOOD. We were taking a little nap, that's all -!
ANITA. And the curtain was pulled back without warning and this ... horrible little man rushed in with a sticker and pasted it on the window!

(The PORTER enters on the run.)

PORTER. Conductor! Conductor! He's at it again! He's on the loose!
CONDUCTOR. I just heard.
PORTER. He's up and down the aisles with those stickers like a phantom!
ANITA. Are we in danger?!
CONDUCTOR. Not in the least, Madam. He's being taken off at Toledo, and we'll be there in just ten minutes. Porter, escort this lady and gentleman to their compartment and see that they're made comfortable.
PORTER. Yes, sir!

(WEBB enters, beaming like a Cheshire cat.)

DR. LOCKWOOD. That's very nice of you. Come along, dear.

ANITA. Our lives aren't safe with that creature running loose.

CONDUCTOR. I assure you he's harmless. Just a little crazy, that's all.

(LOCKWOOD, ANITA and the PORTER exit.)

WEBB. Conductor, when do we get to Toledo?

CONDUCTOR. We'll be in Toledo in 7 minutes. He hasn't been giving Mr. Jaffe any trouble, has he?

WEBB. Who?

CONDUCTOR. The gentleman in D.

WEBB. *(Happily)* Oh, not in the least. Not our Mr. Clark.

CONDUCTOR. You don't know where he's hiding by any chance?

WEBB. … Hiding? What do you mean hiding? From what?

CONDUCTOR. Well, we're trying to keep it under cover, so as not to alarm the passengers. It's a pretty sad case, all around.

WEBB. God Almighty, man, what are you talking about!

CONDUCTOR. This fella Clark. He's been putting those stickers up.

WEBB. It's a damn lie. He's an executive!

CONDUCTOR. Was an executive. We caught him red-handed. We took a whole satchel of those stickers away from him. Here – just read this telegram. Escaped from some asylum, poor fellow. The authorities are picking him up at Toledo in just five minutes. *(WEBB is staring frog-eyed at the telegram.)* Some sort of religious nut, apparently. Thanks. *(He takes the telegram from the*

benumbed IDA.) Oh, and tell Mr. Jaffe I got those wires off.
WEBB. Oh, my God ...

(Drawing Room B. LILY is pouring over the contract, making notes on it. O'MALLEY is watching her, waiting for her to sign. GEORGE, who has obviously come crawling back to LILY, is standing unhappily by.)

LILY. *(Studying the contract.)* Look at this, George. Mr. Jaffe is offering a car and a chauffeur, as well as my own maid and secretary. You know, I don't think there's been a contract like this before in the history of the theatre.
GEORGE. I don't care what it says. I don't trust him. He's a coward.
LILY. Well this thirty thousand dollars down looks pretty brave to me, George.
GEORGE. I'm telling you, it's a mistake to sign it.
LILY. You're my agent now and nothing more. So be professional.
GEORGE. I'm being professional!
O'MALLEY. Why don't you send that stiff out of here so you can concentrate.
LILY. George, go outside. I'll call you later.
GEORGE. Lily -
LILY. Now! Just go! And stop worrying about the contract.

(GEORGE stamps his foot, turns and exits without a word.)

O'MALLEY. He makes a nice exit.
LILY. That's what Oscar said.

(They share a friendly laugh.)

O'MALLEY. Come on now, old girl. Just sign it. You know you're dying to. Here's the historic quill.

LILY. Oh, I don't know, Owen. Signing another contract with Oscar – it's like jumping off a cliff.

O'MALLEY. Into a lake of gold.

LILY. It will mean spending months with him all over again.

O'MALLEY. And you'll adore every second of it. Can't you see the man's in love with you? He's been pining for you for four years. Now sign this thing while the sap is flowing.

LILY. … All right, I'll do it.

(She takes the pen that OWEN has offered, and is just about to sign the contract ... when GEORGE reenters.)

GEORGE. Lily! Stop!

O'MALLEY. Would you get outa here!

LILY. What do you want?!

GEORGE. I have to talk to you before you sign that contract. Just for a minute.

LILY. George –

GEORGE. Please, Lily. If I ever meant anything to you.

(Beat.)

LILY. Oh, all right. But this better be good. *(She hands O'MALLEY the contract.)* I'll be right back, Owen. Keep it warm for me.

(GEORGE and LILY exit.)

CONDUCTOR. *(Off)* Toledo, now arriving!   Toledo, Ohio,
watch your step!

*(As the train pulls to a stop, WEBB hurries in, emotionally dis-
traught.)*

WEBB. Owen?! Has she signed it?!
O'MALLEY. No, not yet.
WEBB. Damn! Owen, we've been fooled. This fellow Clark
– he's a lunatic. He escaped from an asylum.
O'MALLEY. What fella's that?
WEBB. Clark, our backer! The detectives are coming on
board to capture him!
O'MALLEY. Holy God. Have you told Oscar?
WEBB. Not yet.
O'MALLEY. If I were you, I'd jump off the train.
WEBB. *(In tears.)* It's not fair! He looked so real! I would
have been the big hero!! *(A thought suddenly strikes her.)* Oh my
God, what if Oscar signs a commitment to pay somebody? Like
Ringling or Strauss or somebody? He could go to jail!
O'MALLEY. Do me a favor and just kill yourself. I don't
want to see what he does to you.
WEBB. This could be awful! Quick! Come on!

*(They exit, leaving the door open. LILY reenters from the bedroom,
followed by GEORGE.)*

LILY. How dare you talk to me as though I were your wife or
something. God forbid!
GEORGE. Lily –
LILY. He doesn't want me to see Mr. Jaffe again. Well guess

what, George. I'm signing the contract, and so help me God, you
have forced me into it! *(She stops, realizing that O'MALLEY is
gone.)* … Owen … Owen? … Oh, damn, he has the contract.
Thanks a lot, you idiot.

GEORGE. *(Calling after her.)* You're making a mistake!

LILY. … Owen !… Owen?

*(She exits to look for O'MALLEY. GEORGE is alone in the room
for a moment – until the CONDUCTOR and A DETECTIVE
hurry in. They're going through the train room-by-room,
looking for CLARK.)*

DETECTIVE. *(To GEORGE.)* Excuse me, sorry. I'll check
the bedroom.

CONDUCTOR. Good idea.

GEORGE. Hey, what the hell is this?

CONDUCTOR. This is Detective Barnes from the Toledo
Police Department.

DETECTIVE. *(Emerging)* There's nobody there. *(To
GEORGE.)* We're lookin' for a passenger named Clark. He
escaped from some asylum and we're here to collect him.

GEORGE. What's he look like?

DETECTIVE. You can't miss him. He's one of those religious
types. He carries a Bible around all the time and he's always reading it.

*(As the DETECTIVE and the CONDUCTOR exit the room, the
lights go up in A, where JAFFE is reading aloud from the
Bible, declaiming dramatically.)*

JAFFE. "In the beginning was the Word, and the Word was

with God, and the Word was God! In Him was life, and the life was the light of men!" *(The DETECTIVE enters the room and sees him.)* "And behold, an angel of the Lord appeared to Joseph in a dream, saying, "Do not fear to take Mary as your wife, for that which is conceived in her is of the Holy Spirit!"

DETECTIVE. It's him!

(The DETECTIVE leaps forward and grabs JAFFE around the neck in a stranglehold.)

CONDUCTOR. Oh my God!

DETECTIVE. *(Yelling)* I got him! Conductor! He's reading a Bible!

JAFFE. *(Struggling)* What's the meaning of this? Help! Owen! Ida!

CONDUCTOR. Let him go! You're making a mistake!

(The DETECTIVE lets go at last – as O'MALLEY pushes valiantly through, followed by WEBB and LILY.)

O'MALLEY. *(Ready to swing on anybody.)* What's the Hell's going on here …

JAFFE. *(Gurgling)* This man assaulted me!

LILY. What's happening?!

JAFFE. Kill that ruffian, Owen! He broke in and attacked me! Kill him! Kill him!

CONDUCTOR. It's all right, detective. I'll vouch for him. It's Oscar Jaffe, the theatre man.

DETECTIVE. Oh. Sorry, Mr. Jaffe.

CONDUCTOR. Sorry, Mr. Jaffe. They made a mistake.

JAFFE. Well kill him anyway!!!

(The DETECTIVE exits.)

CONDUCTOR. There's a lunatic on board the train and we're trying to track him down.
JAFFE. A lunatic?
CONDUCTOR. A fellow named Clark.
JAFFE. *(A croak.)* … Clark?
CONDUCTOR. That's right. Escaped from an asylum some-place. He had Drawing Room D, but now he's hiding. It's all right, Miss Garland. He's harmless. Nothing to worry about.

(He starts to go.)

LILY. Just a minute, Conductor. Is that Matthew Clark, the patent medicine man?
CONDUCTOR. Yeah, that's him. A really sad case. He pretends to give money away. Writes worthless checks. Apparently it makes him feel better. He thinks he's Jesus Christ or something. It's a funny world.

(The CONDUCTOR exits shaking his head.
Shocked silence.
Then:)

LILY. … Oh, my God!
JAFFE. Lily, it's all news to me. I've been bamboozled …
LILY. *(Raging at OSCAR.)* How dare you lie to me!
JAFFE. I had no idea myself! You've got to believe me!
LILY. You deceitful wretch!
JAFFE. I swear I didn't know!
LILY. Making a fool out of me!

JAFFE. Ida told me he was rich and I believed her! She showed me his card!

LILY. Liar, liar, liar!

JAFFE. *(Reeling and sinking into the seat in a faint.)* Wait a minute, I'm dizzy. Everything's going round and round. Ida, Owen, some water, please. Water …

(He collapses.)

LILY. *(Standing over him and screaming.)* Look who's fainting! You fake! You lunatic! Oh, I can't stand it! Open the window. I can't stand it. I'm going to have a breakdown …

(Train whistle. At this moment, the door opens and MAX JACOBS appears. He's a cigar-chomping producer of the old school.)

JACOBS. Hello, Lily. How's the prettiest girl on ten continents?

JAFFE. Max Jacobs!

(LILY leaps to her feet and throws her arms wildly around MAX'S neck.)

LILY. Oh, Maxie – Maxie! My darling, my sweetheart, my angel …

JACOBS. It's good to see ya, kid. Now listen – I got a new Somerset Maugham play and it fits ya perfect.

JAFFE. What?!

JACOBS. So what do you say? Do we got a deal?

LILY. You bet we do!

JAFFE. *(The howl of a wounded animal.)* NOOOOOOOOO!

(The train pulls out.)

Scene 2

(Drawing Room B. It's almost midnight. MAX JACOBS is chewing on a cigar. GEORGE is listening at the door.)

JACOBS. Leave her alone. Let her finish reading the play. You know, I had a feeling about this whole thing in New York. It came to me all of a sudden, like a bolt of cloth from the blue. "Max Jacobs," I says to myself, "the girl's in trouble. And if you don't act now, you're gonna lose her to that rat-faced, thumb-sucking, pompous jackass Oscar Jaffe." And that's when I was feelin' kindly towards him. So I take a plane to Toledo, one of them small jobs, a pied Piper, and I get on this stinkin' train and I save your bacon! And you call yourself an agent. You're good for nothin'! You got no brains! You got nothin' between the eyes! Cause if you had, you'd a seen this comin' straight at ya like the Three Musketeers of the Apocalypse. And let me tell you something. If Jaffe ever gets her in a show again, you'll lose her for good. Wait. Here she comes.

(The door opens and LILY appears holding a manuscript. She pauses in the doorway to create an entrance.)

LILY. *(Reading the stage directions – then the lines – with utter, utter beauty.)* "Act Three. The last light of the waning moon gutters through the shimmering curtains. Emily struggles to sit up, holding onto the old rocking horse that gave her so much joy as a child. She looks around and there is Jimmy sitting next to her, his eyes swollen with tears and opium." "Oh, Jimmy! What is there to life, that I have not had too much of? Throw all those silly medicines out of the window. I'd like the room to look a bit more like it used to. Like the nursery where we played so happily." (*She lapses into a hurried monotone, reading the hero's part in a mumble, it being of no importance to her.*) Then Jimmy takes me in his arms, gazes into my eyes and says blah blah blah and I say "Darling! I don't need more flowers. Or more sunshine. Or more laughter. You're all the springtime I will ever need!" (*Ditto.*) Then Jimmy starts to cry, sobbing into the blanket murmuring blah blah blah "Oh JIMMY! Poor boy! Please, please don't cry!" (*The grand ending.*) "Jimmy, open the window. Just a little. Oh, is it raining? Soft, warm rain on a sad, broken heart ... Jimmy, how did that little poem go?" (*These are her last words in the play. Uttering them, she dies. Her hand falls, her arms fall, the script falls.*) Oh, God! What a perfect death. So simple. Asking that heart-breaking little question about the poem.

JACOBS. Can you imagine when you sink your chompers into it?

LILY. I haven't been so moved in years. (*To GEORGE, with a sneer, tapping the manuscript.*) Now there's a lover for you, George He knows, he feels, he understands.

GEORGE. I understand.

JACOBS. You understand bupkis! (*To LILY.*) So what's the verdict? Do we go into rehearsal?

LILY. Max, I feel the play was written for me. It is my own life. It has joy. Grief. Tuberculosis. But the second act curtain has to be changed. It is I, not Jimmy, who must make the curtain speech about his wife and children.

JACOBS. No problem. Somerset'll fix it up. Listen, darling, tomorrow we'll go straight from the train to the lawyer's office and draw up the contract. You'll get an advance payment and no nonsense.

LILY. Now that's what I like to hear. Facts.

(During the following, the action cross-fades from Drawing Room B to Drawing Room A.)

GEORGE. But Lily, how much is he paying you?

MAX. I'm paying plenty, that's what I'm paying!

LILY. George, I can take care of myself, thank you.

GEORGE. But this is my job! All right? Now what figure are we talking about here, five a week – ?

MAX. *(Overlapping)* We're talkin' what I say we talk. Cause she trusts me! We go back a long ways!

GEORGE. That's not the point!

(And we're now in Drawing Room A, where JAFFE is talking to the CONDUCTOR.)

JAFFE. Did you have any trouble finding O'Malley and Miss Webb?

CONDUCTOR. No, sir, they were together in the Observation Car.

JAFFE. Good.

CONDUCTOR. But they seemed a bit worse for wear, if you get my meaning.

JAFFE. Drinking?

CONDUCTOR. I'm afraid so.

JAFFE. And did you tell them what I said?

CONDUCTOR. Yes, sir, I told 'em you said it was life and death.

JAFFE. Thank you. I'll call you if I need you.

(The CONDUCTOR exits. JAFFE takes out a revolver, wraps it in a handkerchief, then places the gun and handkerchief in the pocket of his dressing gown. A moment later, the buzzer sounds and O'MALLEY and WEBB enter, both slightly drunk.)

O'MALLEY. The Black Watch, sire. With their bagpipes.

JAFFE. I suppose you're both drunk.

WEBB. *(Snarling)* Drunk or sober, we're here, ain't we?

JAFFE. It's typical of my career that in the great crisis of my life I stand flanked by two incompetent alcoholics.

O'MALLEY. Listen, Oscar, we're in no mood for a lot of fuzzy lamentations.

JAFFE. I won't keep you long, Owen. Just a few words.

WEBB. There's nothing more to say! I've eaten dirt and crawled on my face till I'm sick!

(JAFFE deliberately pulls the handkerchief out of his robe pocket ... and the gun falls to the floor. This is done as if by accident.)

WEBB. Hey, what's that? Is that a gun?!

JAFFE. I'm sorry. I didn't mean for you to see it.

O'MALLEY. *(Hoarsely)* Give me that.

JAFFE. *(Pushing O'MALLEY away.)* No, no. I can see that you've guessed what I called you for. *(He beams tenderly.)* To say goodbye –

WEBB. Owen, stop him!

O'MALLEY. What do you want me to do?!

JAFFE. Do you remember the day not long ago when I was Oscar Jaffe?

WEBB. Would you cut it out?

JAFFE. My outer office was crowded with celebrities. Cabinet Ministers.

O'MALLEY. I ain't listening to a word of this till you put that fowling piece away.

WEBB. For God's sake, let's act like grown-ups for a change.

JAFFE. I know you'll feel blue for a little while, but it's better this way. Yesterday, Oscar Jaffe, the Wizard of Broadway. Tomorrow – a foolish old pest haunting the theatre lobbies on other managers' first nights. *(He grows soft.)* You wouldn't want to see me that way, would you, boys? *(A train whistle. JAFFE looks up at the sound.)* You'll remember me whenever you hear that wild sound in the night.

WEBB. I can't stand it any more, Oscar. You've made me a complete wreck ...

O'MALLEY. This is nuts! I'm leaving!

JAFFE. Goodbye, boys. Come, Pale Messenger of Death – cold passport to heaven or to hell!

(WEBB and O'MALLEY exit and make their way to the Observation Car. At that moment, CLARK enters from the washroom.)

CLARK. Hello ...? *(JAFFE turns and looks at him in surprise. CLARK sees the gun and gasps.)* Oh, dear Heaven. I didn't mean to put the stickers up, it was just overwhelming. Please don't shoot me!

JAFFE. What – ? *(Before JAFFE can say any more, CLARK springs forward and grabs the gun. They struggle over it.)* Stop ... stop ... Stop it!

CLARK. Please don't kill me! Oh, dear God ...!

(BANG! A shot rings out. We see WEBB and O'MALLEY in the Observation car.)

WEBB. Oh, my God!
O'MALLEY. What was that?
WEBB. He's faking! He has to be!

(BANG! BANG! BANG! WEBB and O'MALLEY are frozen in shock – Then they race into Drawing Room A.)

JAFFE. I'm shot!
WEBB. Oscar, why did you do it?
JAFFE. *(Furious)* No! He did it! The lunatic!
CLARK. I'm sorry!

(O'MALLEY and WEBB seize JAFFE and lead him to a chair.)

WEBB. Oh my God!
O'MALLEY. Hold on.
WEBB. Where did he shoot you?!
JAFFE. Near the sofa! God, I'm bleeding!
WEBB. Here, lie down!
O'MALLEY. *(Turning on CLARK.)* Gimme that gun!
WEBB. I'll get a doctor! Don't move!

(She rushes out.)

CLARK. He had the gun and was pointing it at me! It was his life or mine!
JAFFE. He grabbed it away and shot me!
CLARK. It was self-defense!

O'MALLEY. Shut up! Stay right there!

JAFFE. Oh, God, I can see my obituary. "Oscar Jaffe. Killed by lunatic. Also produced plays."

O'MALLEY. *(Adjusting a pillow.)* Listen, Oscar. Do you need a rabbi or a briss or somethin' …?

JAFFE. No. No prayers. I'll plead my own cause before God.

O'MALLEY. *(Hysterical in his own way.)* Don't talk like that. They can't stop you. You'll be on your feet in no time, you old wounded lion. You'll be up at the count of nine.

(WEBB enters at a run.)

WEBB. I've got a doctor. He's coming. How is he? Is he breathing? *(CLARK slides over for a peek at his victim.)* Keep away from him, you!

CLARK. I'm so ashamed!

JAFFE. Please. Don't go away from me now …

O'MALLEY. Never!

WEBB. I'll do anything you say, I promise!

(LOCKWOOD, ANITA, and the CONDUCTOR appear.)

DR. LOCKWOOD. What's the matter?

ANITA. What happened?

CONDUCTOR. Here's the doctor.

WEBB. Quick, Doc – he's dying!

O'MALLEY. Keep everybody out!

CONDUCTOR. Stay back! Keep out of the way!

ANITA. Who shot him?!

CONDUCTOR. Everybody back. Keep this hall clear.

(The lights come up so that we're able to see what's happening in all three rooms.

In Drawing Room B, GEORGE stands in the doorway, listening. People are running back and forth in the hall. LILY enters in a negligee.)

LILY. George, what's happened?

GEORGE. I think there's been an accident.

(MAX enters from the hall.)

LILY. Max, what is it?

JACOBS. *(Happily)* Jaffe's been shot!

LILY. What? *(She screams, then rushes frantically to the door.)* I have to see him!

MAX. *(Stopping her)* No – stay here – stay here – you can't do any good.

LILY. Max, let me go!! Let me go!! I've got to see him!! Max, please –!! Oscar! Oscar!!

(Meanwhile, in Drawing Room A, LOCKWOOD is finishing his examination of JAFFE'S wound. O'MALLEY and WEBB stand anxiously by.)

DR. LOCKWOOD. I'm not surprised. This is often the case. A lot of excitement but no damage.

O'MALLEY. Then it's not serious?

DR. LOCKWOOD. The bullet barely grazed him.

JAFFE. What are you talking about?

DR. LOCKWOOD. You're fit as a fiddle. No damage at all.

JAFFE. But I'm weak. It must be internal injuries. What about all the blood?!

DR. LOCKWOOD. A grazing will often do that. You see, there are blood vessels near the surface –

WEBB. I don't believe it! This is, without a doubt, the worst I've ever been through –

JAFFE. Wait!

O'MALLEY. What?

JAFFE. I have an idea …

WEBB. Oscar –

JAFFE. No, not just an idea – an inspiration!

WEBB. & O'MALLEY. Oscar!

JAFFE. Quiet! Doctor, I want to play a little joke on someone. You can help me.

DR. LOCKWOOD. Well, I don't know if -

JAFFE. I know you have a sense of humor. I know that from your magnificent manuscript for "Joan of Arc," which I have practically decided to produce.

DR. LOCKWOOD. You have? Oh my God! What do you want me to do?

JAFFE. Just sit over there and watch me and say nothing. Ida, where is Lily's contract?

WEBB. What?

JAFFE. The contract. She's going to sign it.

WEBB. Oscar, please –

JAFFE. No. She loves me. I could tell from her screaming. Somehow, I've got to reach that love. Bring her to her senses. Boys, it's the last thing I'll ever ask you to do. Owen, go tell her I'm dying. And don't overact.

O'MALLEY. Stand by, I'll get her. It's a Jaffe Production.

(He hurries out.)

JAFFE. Conductor, set that chair center. No. Just a little off-center. There. Good. And the lights. Down, please. And a little music …*(The CONDUCTOR turns on the radio and we hear something melodramatic.)* Like the last act of Camille.

(JAFFE sits in the chair, pulls a blanket over his legs and leans back as though death is imminent, his face pale, his mouth hanging open.)

O'MALLEY. *(Offstage)* It's all right. Mr. Jaffe wants to see her.
CONDUCTOR. Keep back. Nobody comes in here.
O'MALLEY. It's his last request. Make way for Miss Garland.
WEBB. Let 'em through.

(LILY and O'MALLEY enter.)

LILY. Oscar. … Oscar!

(She sits on the pouffe next to the chair and tries to hold him. JAFFE valiantly tries to raise his head and open his eyes. But it's hard, hard … His voice is thin and distant.)

JAFFE. Who is that?
OWEN. It's Lily.
JAFFE. Bring her to me …
LILY. I'm right here, Oscar. Oh my God! *(She starts to cry; real tears; she thinks he's dying.)* Oh, Oscar! I'm here. It's Lily. I'm right here, my darling. I'm right here. Please don't leave me …
WEBB. The doctor says the bullet went right through his heart so he can't talk much.

JAFFE. Who's that crying?

O'MALLEY. It's Lily.

JAFFE. *(The "mists of death" about him.)* Lily – Lily. Where is your hand? Give me your hand.

LILY. Why did you do it? How could you do this terrible thing?

JAFFE. It's for the best, Lily. There was nothing left. They all went away. Those I loved and needed. It's getting dark. Stay just a little while longer.

LILY. I will. I promise.

(She cries hysterically.)

JAFFE. Dear, lovely Lily. No tears, please. It's not your fault. I only wish I could have seen you, held you, just once more. Ida, where's the contract? The last one I drew up for Lily Garland.

WEBB. Here it is.

JAFFE. Oh, it's so hard to die in this barren place. I should have waited until I got back in the theatre – among the dust and echoes that we loved so well. Ida?

WEBB. Yes?

JAFFE. The contract?

WEBB. It's right here.

JAFFE. Ask her if she would care to write her name on it. That will be my monument.

WEBB. Go on, Lily. It's his last request.

LILY. Yes, yes, give it to me.

WEBB. Here.

O'MALLEY. Here's the pen.

(They give her the contract and the pen. LILY starts signing it. Note, the contract is quadruplicate, four sheets, with a staple

at the top. So after Lily signs the top page, WEBB turns to the next and Lily signs that, too. Then the next; and then the next.)

JAFFE. Hurry, hurry. Give it to me while I can still see. I want to read her name on it.

(Just as she finishes signing, MAX JACOBS rushes in from the corridor.)

JACOBS. Hey, let me through! I'm Max Jacobs! Lily, don't sign the contract!
JAFFE. *(Jumping up and brandishing the signed contract in utter glee)* You're too late, Max Jacobs! Ha haaaaa!

(JACOBS stops cold. Then he rushes at JAFFE in a rage.)

JACOBS. You son of a bitch!
JAFFE. Herring salesman!

(The two men struggle, screaming at each other.)

JACOBS. Thief!
JAFFE. Liar!
JACOBS. Cheat!
JAFFE. Office Boy! ... AHHHHHHHHHH! My leg! Get him off me!!!

(O'MALLEY pulls JACOBS off. LOCKWOOD and the CONDUCTOR look on aghast. And LILY screams – a sound that's echoed instantly by the whistle of the train. And as the curtain falls, LILY walks deliberately towards JAFFE and gives him a right to the jaw, which sends him sprawling.

The lights fade quickly, and in the darkness we hear, first, the noise of the train speeding ahead. Then the train slows down and we hear it pulling into Grand Central Station in New York. We hear the brakes squeal and the bells ring; then we hear the voices of the Red Caps and newsboys:)

VOICES. Red Cap!/Watch your step!/ Stand back for the train!/Need a Red Cap, lady?!

ANNOUNCER. *(On loud speaker.)* The Twentieth Century Limited, now arriving New York City, Track 27! Twentieth Century, on time!

Scene 3

(Outside the Twentieth Century gate, Grand Central Station. The first ones we see emerging from the platform are the CONDUCTOR and the PORTER.)

CONDUCTOR. The Twentieth Century Limited, now arriving New York City, Track 27! Twentieth Century, on time!

PORTER. In a way, I thought the trip was kind of ... well, exciting. You know? Sort of kept me on my toes. Of course it was my first time. Is it always this lively?

CONDUCTOR. Only with the big celebrities. When we had the Marx Brothers I couldn't leave the train at the end, they had my trousers.

(As the PORTER exits, DR. LOCKWOOD and ANITA enter from the train.)

DR. LOCKWOOD. Come on, hurry. We better take separate cabs to the hotel.

ANITA. Grover, this is New York. Nobody worries about sex in New York. They just have it all the time.

DR. LOCKWOOD. I can't believe that Jaffe is producing a play by Somerset Maugham instead of me. It shows he has no taste at all.

ANITA. I still don't get it. You told me that he and Max Jacobs are rivals.

DR. LOCKWOOD. They are. But when Jaffe got Miss Garland to sign his contact, he had her all tied up. The only way Jacobs could get her back was to give Jaffe 50% of the Maugham play. So now they're co-producers. It was blackmail. They're all crooks.

ANITA. And you want to get into this business?

DR. LOCKWOOD. Desperately.

(As they exit, MAX JACOBS and GEORGE emerge. GEORGE is talking as they enter.)

JACOBS. You're complaining! Look at what I lose. Fifty percent of the Maugham play. And now I've got to buy a cage for an ibis.

(As they exit:)

GEORGE. I can't believe she's leaving me like this. She's my Cupid, my Venus, my Hermaphrodite...

(WEBB and O'MALLEY enter.)

O'MALLEY. *(To the CONDUCTOR.)* Is the car ready?
CONDUCTOR. What car?
WEBB. To take Mr. Jaffe to the hotel.
JAFFE. *(Off)* Hotel?! Don't be insane! It's straight to the theatre!!

*(JAFFE. enters. LILY is beside him, dressed to the nines, beaming
    happily. The moment they enter, flashbulbs start popping like
    mad and a bevy of REPORTERS start begging for their atten-
    tion. LILY and JAFFE eat it up.)*

REPORTERS. *(Offstage)* There they are! It's them! Over here,
Miss Garland! Mr. Jaffe, this way! Hold still! You look great!

JAFFE. Hello, boys!
LILY. Did you miss me, fellas?!
REPORTER ONE. Hey Miss Garland – how'd you like
Hollywood?
LILY. Well, you know what they say. It's a place where they
shoot too many pictures and not enough actors.
JAFFE. Now listen, boys, I've got an exclusive for you. I'm
producing a new play on Broadway this season by Somerset
Maugham, with stage effects by John Ringling and music by
Richard Strauss. Most important, it stars this country's greatest
actress, Miss Lily Garland.
REPORTERS AND PHOTOGRAPHERS. No kidding!
Wow! That's great!

(Cameras are flashing through the next exchange.)

JAFFE. We are back together again! Like Beatrice and
Benedict. King Arthur and Queen Guinevere.

LILY. Cesare and Lucrezia Borgia.
OWEN. *(To the reporters.)* OK, thanks, fellas!
JAFFE. Thanks, boys! See you at the opening!

(The reporters exit.)

LILY. By the way, I want Chanel to design all my costumes.
JAFFE. We use Schiaparelli this time.
LILY. Darling, you know nothing about fashion.
JAFFE. I merely created your entire look.
LILY. You don't even know Schiaparelli.
JAFFE. I invented Schiaparelli! Her name was Ethel Bumstein from Altoona, Pennsylvania!
LILY. Oh, stop it! Don't be an –!

(He stops her mouth with a kiss.)

O'MALLEY. Just like old times.
WEBB. Ain't it wonderful
JAFFE. *(Offering his arm.)* To the theatre?
LILY. To the theatre.

(CLARK puts his hear around the corner of the happy couple.)

CLARK. Hallelujah!

(Blackout.)

END OF PLAY

Costume Plot

Beard
    2 pc. Suit
    Shirt/tie
    Shoes

Max Jacobs
    2 pc. Suit
    Shirt/tie
    Overcoat/hat
    Gloves

Porter
    White period coats
    Black tux pants
    Black shoes

Conductor
    Blue uniform suit 3 pc.
    Shirt/tie/shoes

Matthew Clark
    3 pc. Suit
    Shirt/tie/shoes
    Overcoat/bowler hat

Dr. Lockwood
    3 pc. Suit
    Shirt/tie/shoes
    Overcoat/hat/scarf
    Robe/pj's/slippers

Anita

Fur/purse/gloves/hat
Dress/shoes
Nightgown/robe/slippers

Dectective

Trench coat/hat/scarf
3-pc. Suit
Shirt/tie/shoes

Oscar

3 pc. Suit
Tie
Overcoat/scarf/hat
Shoes/blk oxfords

Velvet Robe
Cotton Pajamas
Velvet slippers

Lily

Brown 2 pc. Suit w/halter blouse
Overcoat/hat/fur
Gloves/purse
Shoes

Red Chinese robe
Red Mules

Beaded gown
Peter Fox shoes

Black jumpsuit
Black shoes

Beige Teddy
Beige robe

White coat/dress
White hat
Purse/gloves/shoes

Ida
Overcoat
Hat/gloves/purse
2 pc. Suit
Scarf

Owen
Overcoat/hat
2 pc. Suit
Shirt/tie/shoes

George
2 pc. Suit
Shirt/tie
Overcoat/hat
Shoes

Property Plot
Act I Preset

Item	Preset/Notes
Set Pieces	
Train locked	arm SR, not US
Set truck	set SL/Cabin B offstage
Sliders	open
DS mics	uncovered/no cups
Lounge Car	
Escape platform	ON
Exit door	closed; DOOR KNOB CHECKED
Side chair	DR
Club chair	UR/on spike
Carpet sweeper	DC
Sofa	UC
Wisk broom	on seat; Maid
Side tables (2)	either side of love seat
Ashtrays (2) w/ gel (SL)	1 on top, US end of each table
Sat. Evening Posts	top SL table, top SR pile
Magazines	pile on each shelf
Windows (4)	CLEAN
Pulldown shades	UP
Glass wall	CLEAN
Built-in table	UL
Club chair	SL/on spike
Footstool	on spike
Standing ashtray	DL/on spike
Hallway	
Pulldown shades	UP
Bathroom escape door	closed, not sticking

Compartment A

Built-in writing desk

Blotter	SL
Desk lamp	UR
Ashtray w/ gel	UC
Back-up matchbox	UL
Cups & saucers (2)	DS; handles US
Water tray	
Pitcher w/ water	handle SL
glass	
Tray #1w/sugar dish	SR
Pot w/coffee	DS; handle SL
Vase w/flower&water	SL
Desk chair	seat facing 7:00
Coat closet	empty, door closed/not sticking
Shelf	empty
Hooks	splayed out
Bathroom door	Closed; CHECK DOORKNOB
Box of tissues	DS wall
Towel racks & baskets	
Full length mirror	SL side; clean
Compartment door	closed; CHECK DOORKNOB
Bench Banquette	clear
Coat hooks	empty

Compartment B

Crossover door to A	closed; CHECK DOORKNOB
Bench Banquette	clear
Compartment door	closed; CHECK DOORKNOB
Countertop	UL
Tray	SR
Cham. bucket w/ ice	
Bottle w/ liquid	open
wrap	
Cham. glasses (2)	

Ashtray w/ gel	L of tray
Back-up matchbox	US of ashtray
Train rack	empty
Coat hooks	empty
Club chair	DL, on spike
Exit door (SL)	closed; CHECK DOORKNOB
Escape platform	ON
Light unit for door	ON; cabled

DL

Suitcases, leopard (2)	Red cap (Lily)
Suitcases, tan (2)	Red cap (Lily)
Flower arrangements (3)	Florist (Lily)
Trunk, hat box, flowers on handtruck	Red cap (Lily); by QC booth
Cup w/cig, lighter, water	in QC booth
QC booth sides down, tied back, lx on	

SL Prop Table
Water pitchers, cups, tissues, first aid, Ricola, Cinnamon Altoids

Act I

Suitcase	Porter (D. Dauchan)
Suitcase	Lockwood
Suitcases (2)	Anita
Doctor's bag	Lockwood
Hankie	
Top open attaché	Clark
Pad of stickers, static (4)	
Business cards (5)	in pocket
Briefcase	George
Paramount contract	
Valise	George (Lily)
Academy Award Statue	
Telegram from Clark nephew	Conductor

Double-sided sticker	Conductor
Tickets (2)	Lockwood (pocket)
$1 bill	Lockwood (pocket)
Bible #1 w/sticker (static)	Clark/inside front cover
$1 bill	Clark (pocket)
Business cards (cream)	Clark (pocket)
"Joan of Arc" script, tied	Lockwood
$20 bill	George (pocket)
Cigarette case w/9 cigs	Lily/smokes Camel Lights
Lighter	George (Lily)
Newspaper	Oscar
Plaid hankie	Beard
Cane	Oscar

Act II

Hankie (folded)	Porter
Star contract (4 pp.)	Ida./in purse at Int.; onion paper
$300,000 check	Clark (pocket)
Box of stickers	
1 static, 1 sticky	face to face, sticky on top
Telegrams (written, 10ish)	Oscar/set in Room A at Int.
Business card (cream)	Oscar/set in Room A at Int.
Revolver w/ hankie	Oscar/set in closet at Int.
Bloody hankie	Oscar/set in hall at Int.
Weighted flask	Owen
Telegram pad (all pages blank)	Conductor
Passion Play manuscripts (2)	Beard
Portfolio w/ Script	Max
"Somerset Maugham"	Lily

UC

Platform units (2)	joined
Ground row	joined
LaSalle column & sign	IN; no light fixture
Scrim	to train height

Luggage shelves (3)
    Luggage pile (30 pieces)   STABLE
Fogger   SR spikes
Grand Central Station unit
    Luggage hand truck   SR; Porter

SR Prop Table
Water pitchers, cups, tissues, first aid, Ricola
Dan's towels

Act I

Suitcases (4)	Red caps (PB, DD, BE)
Suitcases (2)	Owen (Oscar)
Briefcase	Ida (Oscar)
Appointment book	under 1 script
Manuscript	top of pile
Address books (3)	L of "Pile"
Cigarette case w/ 9 cigs	in pocket/smokes Winston Ultra Light
Pen (pop top)	in pocket
Lighter	in pocket; filled
Pencils (3)	in pockets
Luggage tags (30+)	Red cap (P. Boll)
$1 bills (5)	Red cap (D. Dauchan)
Invisible dog leashes (2)	STRAIGHT; S. DeRosa
Telegram from Max in env.	Ida
Tickets (2)	Ida (topcoat pocket)
$20 bill	Ida (topcoat pocket)
$5 bill	Ida (suit pocket)
Flasks w/tea (2)	
Owen (coat pocket)	

Act II

Bucket w/ chamois	Porter (D. Dauchan)
Chamois	Maid
Telegram pad (all pages filled out)	Conductor

Pencil	
Cigars (3) w/o wrapper	Ida & Owen
Zippo	
Business card (white)	Owen
Tray w/ dishes	Porter #2
Reporter pads (2)	Reporters (Boll, Smith)
Pencils (2)	
Bible #2	Clark
Sticker	inside front cover
Flashlights (2) w/fresh batteries	Policemen (Dauchan,Cerveris)
Cameras (3) w/ fresh batteries	Reporters (Dauchan, English, Cerveris)

Personal

Set of keys	Porter (pocket)
Pad in black notebook	Porter (pocket/all pages blank)
Pencil	
Double-sided sticker	Conductor
Purse	Ida
Steno pad	
Pen	
Nail files (2)	
Compact/powder puff	
Notepad/Pen	Owen (coat pocket)
Newspaper, folded	Owen (coat pocket)
Pen (black/silver)	Owen
Wallet	Clark (pocket)
Hankie	Beard (pocket)
Handcuffs	Policeman

Act II Preset

Item	Preset/Notes

SR Prop Table

Bucket full of stickers w/chamois	Porter (D. Dauchan)
Rag	Maid
Wisk broom	Porter (B. English)
Telegrams (filled out)	Conductor
Pencil	
Bible #2	Clark
Cigars (3)	Ida & Owen
Zippo	
Business card (white)	Owen
Tray w/dishes	Porter (D. Dauchan)
Reporter pads & pencils (2)	Reporters
Flashlights (2)	Policemen
Cameras (3)	Reporters

Grand Central Station

Luggage hand truck	SR; Porter
Suitcases (5)	small suitcases w/round on top

SL Prop Table

Box of stickers	Clark
$300,000 check	Clark (pocket)
Telegram from Clark nephew	Conductor (pocket)
Telegram pad (all pages blank)	Conductor
Contract (4 pp.)	Ida
Weighted flask	Owen
Passion Play manuscripts (2)	Beard
Portfolio	Max
Script "Somerset Maugham"	Max (Lily)
Doctor's bag	Lockwood

Set Pieces

Set truck	set C - 1/2 Lounge, Room B ON
Sliders	open

Compartment B

Exit door (SL)	closed; CHECK DOORKNOB
Club chair	on spike
Cig pack & lighter	countertop
Compartment door	closed; CHECK DOORKNOB

STRIKE: George's coat & hat, valise, briefcase, champagne stuff

Compartment A

Crossover door to B	closed; CHECK DOORKNOB
Built-in writing desk	
Appointment book	SL; OPEN
Telegrams	on top
Business card	on top
Pencil & Pen	US
Desk chair	seat facing 7:00
Coat closet	empty, door closed
Ida's coat	on outside hook
Revolver in hankie	on suitcase
Bathroom door	Closed; CHECK DOORKNOB
Compartment door	Closed; CHECK DOORKNOB

STRIKE: Vase & water, briefcase, desktop script, Tray #1, cig butt; Oscar gloves, scarf, hat

Hallway

Bloody hankie	US of bathroom door
Windowshade US of A	OPEN

Lounge Car

Windows (4)	2 SR CLEAN; 2 SL with stickers on

3 SL shades	UP
SR shade	DOWN
Magazines (4)	on ottoman
Exit door (SR)	closed; CHECK DOORKNOB
Escape platform	ON

STRIKE: Stickers (2 SR windows)
RESET: magazines on table shelves, furniture on spike. nothing lying around

UC

Briefcase	SR hallway; George
Platform units (2)	
SL luggage shelf STRUCK	
Column w/ light fixtures	CS
Fogger	SL spikes
GCT masking	IN

Last Checked

Pot w/coffee & hankie	SL prop table; Porter/coffee poured at Int.
Bible	at places; Clark/reset end of Act I

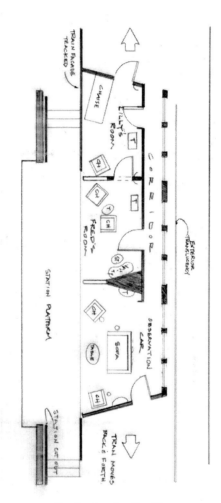

Set Design by Jim Kronzer

TREASURE ISLAND
Ken Ludwig

All Groups / Adventure / 10m, 1f (doubling) / Areas

Based on the masterful adventure novel by Robert Louis Stevenson, *Treasure Island* is a stunning yarn of piracy on the tropical seas. It begins at an inn on the Devon coast of England in 1775 and quickly becomes an unforgettable tale of treachery and mayhem featuring a host of legendary swashbucklers including the dangerous Billy Bones (played unforgettably in the movies by Lionel Barrymore), the sinister two-timing Israel Hands, the brassy woman pirate Anne Bonney, and the hideous form of evil incarnate, Blind Pew. At the center of it all are Jim Hawkins, a 14-year-old boy who longs for adventure, and the infamous Long John Silver, who is a complex study of good and evil, perhaps the most famous hero-villain of all time. Silver is an unscrupulous buccaneer-rogue whose greedy quest for gold, coupled with his affection for Jim, cannot help but win the heart of every soul who has ever longed for romance, treasure and adventure.

CPSIA information can be obtained at www.ICGtesting.com
Printed in the USA
BVOW001104290313

316566BV00018B/284/P